Thank You For The Flowers

Stories of Suspense & Imagination

By Scott Nicholson

to Andrea —
may all your gardens come up
roses — don't be afraid to
go for it! Best Wishes,
Scott Nicholson
11/18/00

Parkway Publishers, Inc
Boone, North Carolina

2000

D1057736

Library of Congress Cataloging-in-Publication Data
Nicholson, Scott, 1962-
    Thank you for the flowers : a story collection / by Scott Nicholson
        p.   cm.
    ISBN 1-887905-24-3
    1. Detective and mystery stories, American. 2. Horror tales,
    American. I. Title
    PS3564.I2796 T48 2000
    813'.6--dc21   00-038559

"Haunted" © 1998   "Do You Know Me Yet?" © 1999
"Skin" © 2000   "Homecoming" © 1998
"The Vampire Shortstop" © 1999   "Kill Your Darlings" © 1998
"Dead Air" © 1998   "Metabolism" © 1998
"In The Heart of November" © 2000   "The Boy Who Saw Fire" © 1998
"The Three-Dollar Corpse" © 1999   "Constitution" © 1999
"Thirst" © 1999   Afterwords © 2000

Cover art by John Shamburger
Graphic Design by Aaron Burleson
Layout by Jamie Goodman

Acknowledgments

Very special thanks to my dear wife and world's greatest proofreader Angela; my mother Delores who always taught her children to be stubbornly persistent; my son Brian who forgives me my writerly musings; Miranda for providing hope for the future; John Shamburger for the beautiful cover painting; Aaron Burleson for the graphic design; Jamie Goodman for the page layout; Kevin J. Anderson for practical advice; Dave Wolverton for fishing me out of the slush; and all friends, fans, and especially you readers who are opening your hearts and minds and lungs to my stories.

TABLE OF CONTENTS

How nice of you to come.

It would have been easy to stay away, to leave me where I lay. Yet you came, even though the moon is low and you really should be asleep, safe in your dreams of silk. You came even though your bones rattle with the chill.

I'm so glad you're here. Now we can have that little chat, lost in darkness with nothing between us. No more lying. No eye games, no distractions, no dreaded tomorrows or forlorn yesterdays to hide behind.

Just you and me and words.

Trust me. Take my hand.

We're in this together, you and I, in this dance of dust and air.

We will walk in shadows, we will learn to breathe again, we will teach our hearts to beat.

Because hope should never surrender, and love should never rest in peace.

So let's go, all the way.

And then some.

Farther.

By the way, thank you for the flowers.

THANK YOU FOR
THE FLOWERS

Haunted

"Do it again, Daddy." Janie's coloring book was in her lap, forgotten.

Darrell smiled and thumbed open the top on his Zippo lighter. He struck the flint wheel and the flame burst to life. The dancing fire reflected in each of Janie's pupils. Her mouth was open in fascination.

"It's pretty," she said.

"And so are you. Now back to your coloring. It's almost bedtime." Darrell flipped the silver metal lid closed, snuffing the orange flame.

Janie put the coloring book in front of her and rolled onto her stomach. She chose a crayon. Gray. Darrell frowned and placed the lighter by the ashtray.

Rita tensed in her chair beside him. She reached out with her thin hand and gripped his arm. "Did you hear that?" she whispered.

Darrell listened. Janie was humming to herself. The wax of the crayon made a soft squeak across the paper. The clock on the mantel ticked once, again, three times, more.

He tried to hear beyond those normal sounds. His hearing was shot. Too much Elvis, Rita always said. Too much Elvis would make anybody deaf.

"From the kitchen," she said. "Or outside."

Janie heard the same noise that Rita was hearing. She cocked her head, the crayon poised above the page. She stopped kicking her feet, the heels of her saddle shoes nearly touching her back.

"Mice, most likely," he said, too loudly. He was head of the household. It was his job to put on a brave face. The expression fit him like a glass mask.

Why didn't the damned dog bark? Dogs were supposed to be sensitive to spirits from the other side. He put down the newspaper, paper crackling. Martin Luther King and Mayor Loeb looked out from the front page. Black and white.

"Terribly loud mice," Rita finally answered. Darrell shot her a glance, then rolled his eyes toward Janie. Rita was usually careful in front of their daughter. But having those noisy things around had been stressful.

"Sounds like it's coming from the kitchen," he said with what he hoped was nonchalance. He pulled his cigar from his mouth. He rarely smoked, and never inside the house. But they were a comfort, with their rich sweet smell and tangy taste and round weight between his lips.

He laid the cigar carefully beside his lighter, propping up the damp end on the ashtray so the dust wouldn't stick to it. The ashtray was shaped like a starfish. They'd gotten it on their honeymoon to Cuba, back when Americans were allowed to visit. He could still see the map of the island that had been painted on the bottom of the glass.

Darrell stood, his recliner groaning in relief. He looked down at the hollow impression in the woven seat of the chair.

Too much food. Too much food, and too much Elvis.

Can't go back. Can't get younger. Can't change things. He shook his head at nothing.

"Don't bother, honey. The mice won't hurt anything." Rita chewed at the red end of her index finger.

"Well, we can't let them have the run of the house." It was their secret code, worked out over the long sleepless night. Janie didn't need to know. She was too young to understand. But the things were beyond anybody's understanding, no matter what age a person was.

Darrell glanced at the big boxy RCA that cast a flickering shadow from one corner of the room. They usually watched with the sound turned down. Barney Fife was saying something to Andy, his Adam's apple twitching up and down like a turkey's.

"Get me a soda while you're up?" Rita asked. Trying to pretend everything was normal.

"Sure. Anything for you, pumpkin?"

Janie shook her head. He wished she would go back to coloring. Her eyes were wide now, waiting. He was supposed to protect her from worries.

She put the gray crayon back in the box. Fifteen other colors, and she almost always used gray. Freud would probably have made something of that. Darrell hoped she would select a blue, even a red, something vibrant and found in rainbows. His heart tightened as she chose black.

He walked past her and turned up the sound on the television. Beginning to whistle, he headed across the living room. No tune came to mind. He forced a few in-between notes and the music jumped track somewhere in his throat. He began again, with "I See the Moon." Janie's favorite.

Where was that dog? Always underfoot when Darrell

went through the house, but now nowhere to be found. Nothing like this ever happened back in Illinois. Only in Tennessee.

He was in the hall when he heard Aunt Bea's aria from the living room: "An-deeeee!"

They used to watch "The Outer Limits," sometimes "The Twilight Zone." Never again. They got too much of that sort of thing in real life. Now it was nothing but safe, family fare.

Darrell eased past the closet. His golf clubs were in there, the three-wood chipped where he'd used it to drive a nail into the kitchen drawer that was always coming apart. Cobwebs probably were stretched between the irons. Par for the course, these days.

He stopped outside the kitchen. A bright rectangle of light spilled into the hallway. Mice were supposed to be scared of house lights. Well, maybe mice were, but those things weren't. Then why did they only come at night?

There was a smudge of fingerprints on the doorway casing. Purple. Small. Grape jelly.

He tried to yawn, but his breath hitched. He checked the thermostat, even though it was early autumn and the temperature was fairly constant. He looked around for another excuse for delay, but found none.

The kitchen floor was off-white linoleum, in a Pollock sort of pattern that disguised scuffs and stains. Mice would find nothing on this floor.

The Formica counters were clean, too. Three soiled plates were stacked in the sink. He didn't blame Rita for avoiding the chore. No one wanted to be alone in the kitchen, especially after dinner when the sun had gone down.

A broom leaned against the little door that hid the folding-out ironing board. He wrapped his hands around the smooth wood. Maybe he could sweep them away, as if they were dust balls.

Darrell crossed the kitchen slowly, the broom held across his chest. As he crouched, he felt the bulge of his belly lapping over his belt. Both he and his crosstown hero were packing on the weight in these later years.

Where was that dog? A few black-and-white clumps of hair stuck to the welcome mat at the back door. That dog shed so much, Darrell wouldn't be surprised if it was invisible by now. But the mess was forgivable, if only the mutt would show up. A good bark would scare those things away.

He parted the curtain on the back door. The grass in the yard had gotten tall and was a little ragged. George next door would be tut-tutting to his wife. But George was retired, he had nothing on his mind but lawn fertilizer. There was a joke in there somewhere, but Darrell wasn't in the mood to dig it up.

A little bit of wind played in the laurel hedge, strong enough to make the seat of Janie's swing set ease back and forth. Of course it was the wind. What would those things want with a swing set? The set's metal poles were flecked with rust. He didn't remember that happening. Gradual changes weren't as noticeable, he supposed.

In the dim light, the world looked colorless. Nothing else stirred. If they were out there, they were hiding. He almost expected to hear some corny organ music like they played on the "Inner Sanctum" radio program.

He was about to drop the curtain and get Rita's soda, and maybe a beer for himself, when he saw movement. Two shapes, wispy and pale in the faded wash of the backyard. Trick of the moonlight. Yeah. Had to be. They didn't exist, did they?

He looked forward to the beer bubbling in his throat.

The bitter sweetness wasn't as crisp as it used to be back when he was young. Maybe everything got flatter and less vivid as a person got older. Senses dulled by time and timelessness.

The big General Electric was nearly empty. The celery had wilted. Something on the middle wire shelf had separated into layers. He didn't dare open the Tupperware container to see what was inside. A half-dozen eggs roosted in their scooped-out places. One had a hairline crack, and a clear jewel of fluid glistened under the fluorescent light.

He fished out the drinks and closed the door. There was a hiss as the motor kicked in and sucked the seals tight. A fluff of lint shot from the grill at the base of the appliance.

The drinks chilled his palms. Sensation. He pressed a can to his forehead. Great way to cure a headache. Too bad he didn't have one.

He went back to the living room. Janie was still coloring, the tip of her tongue pressed just so against the corner of her mouth. Her eyes were half-closed, the curl of her lashes making Darrell's heart ache. He sat down.

Darrell gave Rita the soda, then pulled the tab on his beer. The can opened with a weak, wet sigh. He took a sip. Flat.

"See any mice?" Rita asked, trying to smile.

"Not a single Mickey Mouse in the place. Saw a Donald Duck, though."

Janie giggled, her shoulders shaking a little. Her ponytail had fallen against one cheek. Darrell hated lying. But it wasn't really a lie, was it? The lie was so white, it was practically see-through.

He settled back in his chair. The newspaper had slipped to the floor and opened to page seven, where the real news was located. More stuff on Johnson's mess in Viet Nam. Right now, he had no interest in the world beyond. He looked at the television.

Gomer was doing something stupid, and his proud idiot grin threatened to split his head in half. Barney was waving his arms in gangly hysterics. Andy stood there with his hands in his pockets.

Television was black-and-white, just like life. But in television, you had "problem," then "problem solved." Sprinkle in some canned laughter along the way. In life, there were no solutions and not much laughter.

He took another sip of beer. "You want to visit your folks again this weekend?"

Rita had gulped half her soda in her nervousness. "Can we afford it?"

Could they afford not to? Every minute away from the house was a good minute. He wished they could move. He had thought about putting the house up for sale, but the market was glutted. The racial tension had even touched the midtown area, and middle-class whites didn't want to bring their families to the South. Besides, who would want to buy a haunted house?

And if they did manage to sell the house, where would they go? Shoe store managers weren't exactly in high demand. And he didn't want Rita to work until Janie started school. So they'd just have to ride it out for another year or so. Seemed like they'd been riding it out forever.

He put down the beer and jabbed the cigar in his mouth. "Maybe your folks are getting tired of us," he said around the rolled leaf. "How about a trip to the mountains? We can get a little cabin, maybe out next to a lake." He thought of his fishing rod, leaning against his golf bag somewhere in the lost black of the closet.

"Out in the middle of nowhere?" Rita's voice rose a half-step too high. Janie noticed and stopped scribbling.

"We could get a boat."

"I'll call around," Rita said. "Tomorrow."

Darrell looked at the bookcase on the wall. He'd been meaning to read so many of those books. He wasn't in the mood to spend a few hours with one. Even though he had all the time in the world.

He picked up the Zippo and absently thumbed the flame to life. Janie heard the lid open and looked up. Pretty colors. Orange, yellow, blue. He doused the flame, thumbed it to life once more, then closed the lighter and put it back on the table.

Rita pretended to watch television. Darrell looked from her face to the screen. The news was on, footage of the sanitation workers' strike. The reporter's voice-over was bassy and bland.

"Do you think it's serious?" Rita asked, with double meaning.

"A bunch of garbage." The joke fell flat. Darrell went to the RCA and turned down the volume. Silence crowded the air.

Janie stopped coloring, lifted her head and cocked it to one side. "I heard something."

Her lips pursed. A child shouldn't suffer such worry. He waited for a pang of guilt to sear his chest. But the guilt was hollow, dead inside him.

"I think it's time a little girl went beddy-bye," he said. Rita was standing before he even finished his sentence.

"Aw, do I have to?" Janie protested half-heartedly.

"Afraid so, pumpkin."

"I'll go get the bed ready, then you can come up and get brushed and washed," Rita said, heading too fast for the stairs.

"And Daddy tells the bedtime story?" Janie asked.

Darrell smiled. Rita was a wonderful mother. He couldn't imagine a better partner. But when it came to telling stories, there was only one king. "Sure," he said. "Now gather your crayons."

The promise of a story got Janie in gear. Darrell heard Rita's slippered feet on the stairs. Her soles were worn. He'd have to get her a new pair down at the store.

He froze, the hairs on his neck stiffening.

There.

That sound again.

The not-mice.

Where was that damn dog?

He got to his feet, stomach clenched. Janie was preoccupied with her chore. He walked to the back door and parted the curtain, wondering if Rita had heard and was now looking out from the upstairs window.

The moon was fuller, brighter, more robust. Why did they only come at night?

Maybe they had rules. Which was stupid. They broke every natural law just in the act of existing.

There, by the laurel at the edge of the backyard. Two shapes, shimmering, surreal, a bit washed out.

He opened the door, hoping to scare them away. That was a hoot. Him scaring them. But he had to try, for Janie's and Rita's sake.

"What do you want?" he said, trying to keep his voice level. Could they understand him? Or did they speak a different language in that other world?

The shapes moved toward him, awkwardly. A bubbling sound flooded the backyard, like pockets of air escaping from water. One of the shapes raised a nebulous arm. The motion was jerky, like in an old silent film.

Darrell stepped off the porch. Maybe if he took a stand here, they would take what they wanted and leave his family alone.

"There's nothing for you here," he said. "Why don't you go back where you came from?"

A sudden rage flared through him, filling his abdomen with heat. These were the things that bothered Janie, that made Rita worry, that was the fountain of his own constant guilt. These things had no right to intrude on their space, their lives, their reality.

"I don't believe in you," he shouted, no longer caring if he woke Neighbor George. If only the dog would bark, maybe that would drive them away.

The bubbling sound came again. The spooks were closer now, and he could see they were shaped like humans. Noises from their heads collected and hung in the air. The wind lifted, changed direction. The noises blew together, thickened and became words.

Darrell's language.

"There's where it happened."

A kid. Sounded like early teens. Did their kind age, or were they stuck in the same moment forever?

Darrell opened his mouth, but didn't speak. More words came from the world of beyond, words that were somnambulant and sonorous.

"Gives me the creeps, man." Another young one.

"Three of them died when it burned down."

"Freaky. Maybe some of the bones are still there."

"They say only the dog got away."

"Must have been a long time ago."

"Almost thirty years."

"Nothing but a chimney left, and a few black bricks. You'd think something would grow back. Trees and stuff." A silence. Darrell's heart beat, again, three times, more.

"It's supposed to be haunted," said the first.

"Bullshit."

"Go out and touch it, then."

"No way."

A fire flashed in front of one of the shapes, then a slow curl of smoke wafted across the moonlit yard. The end of a cigarette glowed. Smoke. Spirit. Smoke. Spirit. Both insubstantial.

Darrell walked down the back steps, wondering how he could make them go away. A cross? A Bible? A big stick?

"I only come here at night," said the one inhaling the fire.

"Place gives me the creeps."

"It's cool, man."

"I don't like it." The shape drifted back, away from the house, away from Darrell's approach.

"Chicken."

The shape turned and fled.

"Chicken," repeated the first, louder, sending a puff of gray smoke into the air.

Darrell glanced up at Janie's bedroom window. She would be in her pajamas now, the covers up to her chin, a picture book across her tummy. The pages opened to a story that began "Once upon a time..."

Darrell kept walking, nearing the ghost of shifting smoke and fire. He was driven by his anger now, an anger that drowned the fear. The thing didn't belong in their world. Everything about them was wrong. Their bad light, their voices, their unreal movement.

He reached out, clutching for the thing's throat. His hands passed through the flame without burning, then through the shape without touching. But the shape froze, shuddered, then turned and fled back to its world of beyond.

Darrell watched the laurels for a moment, making sure the thing was gone. They would come back. They always did. But tonight he had won. A sweat of tension dried in the gentle breeze.

He went inside and closed the door. He was trembling. But he had a right to feel violated, outraged. He hadn't invited the things to his house.

He had calmed down a little by the time he reached the living room. A Spencer Tracy movie was on the television. The glow from the screen flickered on the walls like green firelight.

Rita was in her chair, blinking too rapidly. "Was it...?" she asked.

"Yeah."

"Oh, Darrell, what are we going to do?"

"What can we do?"

"Move."

He sighed. "We can't afford to right now. Maybe next year."

He sat down heavily and took a sip of his beer. It was still flat.

"What do we tell Janie?"

"Nothing for now. It's just mice, remember?"

He wished the dog were here, so he could stroke it behind the ears. He thought of those words from beyond, and how they said something about the dog getting out. Getting out of what?

He reached for his cigar and stuck it in his mouth. After a moment, he said, "Maybe if we stop believing in them, they'll go away."

The clock ticked on the mantel.

"I can't," Rita said.

"Neither can I."

The clock ticked some more.

"She's waiting."

"I know."

Darrell leaned his cigar carefully against the ashtray. He noticed his lighter was missing. He shrugged and went upstairs to read Janie her story. He wondered if tonight the ending would be the same as always.

The Vampire Shortstop

Jerry Shepherd showed up at first practice alone.

I mean, *showed*, as if he'd just popped into thin air at the edge of the woods that bordered Sawyer Field. Most kids, they come to first practice book-ended by their parents, who glower like Mafia heavies willing to break your kneecaps if their kid rides the pine for so much as an inning. So in a way, it was a relief to see Jerry materialize like that, with no threat implied.

But in another way, he made me nervous. Every year us Little League coaches get handed two or three players who either recently moved to the area or were given their release (yeah, we're that serious here) by their former teams. And if there's one thing that's just about universal, it's the fact that these Johnny-come-latelies couldn't hit their way out of a paper bag. So I figured, here's this spooky kid standing there at the fence, just chewing on his glove, real scared-like, so at least there's one brat who's not going to be squealing for playing time.

I figured him for a vampire right off. He had that pale

complexion, the color of a brand new baseball before the out-field grass scuffs up the horsehide. But, hey, these are enlight-ened times, everybody's cool with everybody, especially since "Transylvania" Wayne Kazloski broke the major league undead barrier back in '29. And that old myth about vampires melting in the sun is just that, an old myth.

The league powers figured I wouldn't raise a fuss if they dumped an undesirable on me. I had eleven kids on the roster, only five of them holdovers from the year before, so I was start-ing from scratch anyway. I didn't mind a new face, even if I was pretty much guaranteed that the vampire kid had two left feet. Coming off a three-and-thirteen season, the Maynard So-lar Red Sox didn't have any great expectations to live up to.

All the other players had clustered around me as if I were giving out tickets to see a rock band, but Jerry just hung out around first base like a slow-thawing cryogenic.

"I'm Coach Ruttlemyer," I said, loudly enough to reach Jerry's pointy ears. "Some of you guys know each other and some of you don't. But on my team, it's not who you know that counts, it's how hard you play."

At this point in the first preseason speech, you always catch some kid with a finger in his or her nose. That year, it was a sweet-faced, red-headed girl. She had, at that moment, banished herself to right field.

"Now, everybody's going to play in every game," I said. "We're here to have fun, not just to win."

The kids looked at me like they didn't buy that line of bull. I barely believed it myself. But I always said it extra-loud so that the parents could hear. It gave me something to fall back on at the end of a lousy season.

"We're going to be practicing hard because we only have two weeks before the first game," I said, pulling the bill of my cap down low over my eyes so they could see what a serious guy I was. "Now let's see who's who."

I went down the roster alphabetically, calling out each player's name. When the kid answered "Here," I glanced first at the kid, then up into the bleachers to see which parents were grinning and straining their necks. That's a good way to tell right off who's going to want their kid to pitch: the beefy, red-faced dad wearing sunglasses and too-tight polyester shorts, and the mom who's busy organizing which parent is bringing what snack for which game.

When I called out Jerry's name, he croaked out a weak syllable and grimaced, showing the tips of his fangs. I waved him over to join the rest of the team. He tucked his glove in his armpit and jogged to the end of the line. I watched him out of the corner of my eye, waiting for him to trip over the baseline chalk. But he didn't stumble once, and that's when I got my first glimmer of hope that maybe he'd be able to swipe a couple of bases for me. He was gaunt, which means that if he's clumsy you call him "gangly," but if he's well-coordinated you call him "sleek." So maybe we're not as enlightened as we claim to be, but hey, we're making progress.

I liked to start first practice by having the kids get on the infield dirt and snag some grounders. You can tell just about everything you need to know about a player that way. And I don't mean just gloving the ball and pegging it over to first. I mean footwork, hand-eye, hustle, aggressiveness, vision, all those little extras that separate the cellar-dwellers from the also-rans from the team that takes home the Sawyer Cup at the end of the season. And it's not just the way they act when it's their turn; you get a lot of clues by how they back each other up, whether they sit down between turns, whether they punch each other on the arm or hunt for four-leaf clovers.

By the first run through, ten ground balls had skittered through to the deep grass in centerfield. But one, <u>one</u>, made up for all those errors. Jerry Shepherd's grounder. He skimmed the ball off the dirt and whizzed it over to first as if the ball were a yo-yo and he held the string. My assistant coach and darling wife Dana grinned at me when the ball thwacked into her mitt. I winked at her, hoping the play wasn't a fluke.

But it was no fluke. Six turns through, and six perfect scoops and tosses by Jerry Shepherd. Some of the other kids were fifty-fifty risks, and one, you'd have guessed the poor little kid had the glove on the wrong hand. You know the kind, parents probably raised him on computer chess and wheat bran. Oops, there I go again, acting all unenlightened.

Another bright spot was Elise Stewart, my best returning player. She only made the one error on her first turn, and I could chalk that up to a long winter's layoff. She was not only sure-handed, she was also the kind of girl you'd want your son to date in high school. She had a happy heart and you just knew she'd be good at algebra.

All in all, I was pleased with the personnel. In fifteen years of coaching Little League, this was probably the best crop of raw talent that I'd ever had. Now, I wasn't quite having delusions of being hauled out of the dugout on these guys' shoulders (me crushing their bones and hoisting the Sawyer Cup over my head), but with a little work, we had a chance at a winning season.

I made a boy named Biff put on the catcher's gear and get behind the plate. In baseball films, the chunky kid always plays catcher, but if you've ever watched even one inning of a real Little League game, you know the catcher needs to be quick. He spends all his time against the backstop, stumbling over his mask and jerking his head around looking for the baseball.

Besides, Biff had a great name for a catcher, and what more could you ask for?

I threw batting practice, and again each kid had a turn while the others fanned out across the diamond. I didn't worry as much about hitting as I did fielding, because I knew hitting was mostly a matter of practice and concentration. It was a skill that could be taught. So I kind of expected the team to be a little slow with the bat, and they didn't disappoint me.

Except when Jerry dug into the batter's box. He stared at me with his pupils glinting red under the brim of his batting helmet, just daring me to bring the heat. I chuckled to myself. I liked this kid's cockiness at the plate. But I used to be a decent scholarship prospect, and I still had a little of the old vanity myself. So instead of lobbing a cream puff, I kicked up my leg and brought the Ruttlemyer Express.

His line drive would have parted my hair, except for two things: I was wearing a cap and my hairline barely reached above my ears. But I felt the heat off his scorcher all the same, and it whistled like a bullet from a gun. I picked up the rosin bag and tossed it in the air a few times. Some of the parents had stopped talking among themselves and watched the confrontation.

Jerry dug in and Biff gave me a target painting the black on the inside corner. I snapped off a two-seamer curveball, hoping the poor batter didn't break his spine when he lunged at the dipping pitch. But Jerry kept his hips square, then twisted his wrists and roped the ball to right field for what would have been a stand-up double. I'd never seen a Little Leaguer who could go with a pitch like that. I tossed him a knuckleball, and most grown-ups couldn't have hit it with a tennis racket, but Jerry drilled it over the fence in left-center.

Okay. *Okay.*

He did miss one pitch and hit a couple of fouls during his turn. I guess even vampires are only human.

After practice, I passed out uniforms and schedules and talked to the parents. I was hoping to tell Jerry what a good job he'd done and how I'd be counting on him to be a team leader, but he snatched up his goods and left before I had the chance. He got to the edge of the woods, then turned into a bat (the flying kind, not the kind you hit with) and flitted into the trees, his red jersey dangling from one of his little claws. His glove weighed him down a little and he was blind, of course, so he bumped into a couple of tree limbs before he got out of sight.

And so went the two weeks. Jerry was a natural short-stop, even the other kids saw that. Usually, everybody wanted to pitch and play shortstop (both positions at the same time, you know), but nobody grumbled when I said Jerry would be our starting shortstop. Elise was starting pitcher, and Wheat Bran and the redhead were "designated pinch hitters." I told everybody to get a good night's sleep, because we would be taking on the Piedmont Electric Half-Watts, which was always one of the better teams.

I could hardly sleep that night, I was so excited. Dana rolled over at about one A.M. and stole her pillow back.

"What's wrong?" she grunted.

"The game," I said. I was running through lineups in my mind, planning strategies for situations that might arise in the sixth inning.

"Go to sleep. Deadline's tomorrow."

"Yeah, yeah, yeah." I was editor of the *Sawyer Creek E-Weekly*, and Thursday noon was press time. I still had some unfinished articles. "That's just my job, but baseball is my life-blood."

Thinking of lifeblood made me think of Jerry. The poor

kid must have lost his parents. Back a few centuries ago, there had been a lot of purging and staking and garlic-baiting. Yeah, like I said, we're making progress, but sometimes I wonder if you can ever really change the human animal. I hoped nothing would come up about his being a vampire.

I knew how cruel Little League could be. Not the kids. They could play and play and play, making up rules as they went along, working things out. No, it was the parents who sometimes made things ugly, who threw tantrums and called names and threatened coaches. I'd heard parents boo their own kids.

In one respect, I was glad Jerry was an orphan. At least I didn't have to worry about his parents changing into wolves, leaping over the chain-link fence, and ripping my throat out over a bad managerial decision. Not that vampires perpetrated that sort of violence. Still, all myths contain a kernel of truth, and even a myth can make you shiver.

I finally went to sleep, woke up and got the paper online. I drove out to the ballfield and there were four dozens vehicles in the parking lot. There's not much entertainment in Sawyer Creek. Like I said, Little League's a big deal in these parts, plus it was a beautiful April day, with the clouds all puffy and soft in the blue sky. Dana was already there, passing out baseballs so the kids could warm up. I looked around and noticed Jerry hadn't arrived.

"He'll be here," Dana said, reading my nervousness.

We took infield and I was filling out the lineup card when Elise pointed to centerfield. "Hey, looky there, Coach," she said.

Over the fence loped a big black dog, with red socks and white pin-striped pants. Propped between the two stiff ears was a cockeyed cap. The upraised tail whipped back and forth in the breeze, a worn glove hooked over its tip. The dog transformed into Jerry when it got to second base.

A murmur rippled through the crowd. I felt sorry for Jerry then. The world may be enlightened, but the light's a little slower in reaching Sawyer Creek than it is most places. There are always a few bigots around. Red, yellow, black, and white, we had all gotten along and interbred and become one race. But when you get down to the equality of the living and the living dead, some people just don't take to that notion of unity as easily.

And there was something else that set the crowd on edge, and even bothered *me* for a second. Hanging by a strap around his neck was one of those sports bottles all the kids have these days. Most of the kids put in juice or Super-Ade or something advertised by their favorite big leaguers. But Jerry's drink was thick and blood-red. Perfectly blood-red.

"Sorry I'm late," he said, sitting down on the end of the bench. I winced as he squirted some of the contents of the sports bottle into his throat.

"Play ball," the umpire yelled, and Elise went up to the plate and led off with a clean single to right. The next kid bunted her over, then Jerry got up. The first pitch bounced halfway to home plate and Elise stole third. Dana, who was coaching third base, gave her the "hold" sign. I wanted to give Jerry a chance to drive her in.

The next pitch was a little high, but Jerry reached out easily with the bat. The ball dinged off the titanium into center and we were up, one to nothing. And that was the final score, with Elise pitching a three-hitter and Jerry taking away a handful of hits from deep in the hole. Jerry walked once and hit another double, but Wheat Bran struck out to leave him stranded in the fifth.

Still, I was pleased with the team effort, and a "W" is a "W," no matter how you get it. The kids gathered around the snack cooler after the game, all happy and noisy and ready to play soccer or something. But not Jerry. He had slipped away before I could pat him on the back.

"Ain't no fair, you playing a slanty-eyed vampire," came a gruff voice behind me. "Next thing you know, they'll allow droids and other such trash to mix in. Baseball's supposed to be for normal folks."

I turned to find myself face-to-face with Roscoe Turnbull. Sawyer Creek's Mister Baseball. Coach of the reigning champs for the past seven years. He'd been watching from the stands, scouting the opposition the way he always did.

"Hey, he's got just as much right to play as anybody," I said. "I know you're not big on reading, but someday you ought to pick up the U.S. Constitution and check out the 43rd Amendment."

The Red Sox had never beaten one of Turnbull's teams, but at least I could be smug in my intellectual superiority.

"Big words don't mean nothing when they're giving out the Sawyer Cup," Turnbull hissed through his Yogi Berra teeth. He had a point. He'd had to build an addition onto his house just so he could store all the hardware his teams had won.

"We'll see," I said, something I never would have dared to say in previous years. Turnbull grunted and got in his panel truck. His son Ted was in the passenger seat, wearing the family scowl. I waved to him and went back to my team.

We won the next five games. Jerry was batting something like .900 and had made only one error, which occurred when a stray moth bobbed around his head in the infield. He'd snatched it out of the air with his mouth at the same moment the batter sent a three-hopper his way. I didn't say anything. I mean, instincts are instincts. Plus, we were winning, and that was all that mattered.

The seventh game was trouble. I'd been dreading that line on the schedule ever since I realized that my best player was a vampire. Maynard Solar Red Sox versus The Dead Reckoning Funeral Parlor Pall Bearers. Now, no self-respecting parlors were *selling* the blood that they drained. But there had been rumors of underground activity, a black market for blood supplies.

And Jerry had slowly been catching the heat, anyway. The grumbles from the stands had gotten louder, and whenever Jerry got up to bat or made a play in the field, some remark would come from the opposing bleachers. Oh, they were the usual unimaginative kind, like the old "Kill the vampire," the play on the resemblance between the words "vampire" and "umpire." The other common one was "Vampires suck." And these were the parents, mind you. They wonder where kids get it from.

The cruelest one, and the one that caught on the fastest, came from the unlikely mouth of Roscoe Turnbull, who'd made a habit of bringing his son Ted to our games just so they could ride Jerry's case. Jerry had launched a three-run homer to win in the last inning of one of our games. As he crossed the plate, Turnbull yelled out, "Hey, look, everybody. It's the Unnatural." You know, a play on the old Robert Redford film. Even *I* had to grudgingly admit that was a good one.

Now we were playing a funeral parlor and I didn't know where Jerry got his blood. I usually didn't make it my business to keep up with how the kids lived their lives off the diamond. But Jerry didn't have any parents, any guidance. Maybe he could be bribed to throw a game if the enticements were right.

So I was worried when Jerry came to bat in the sixth with two outs. We were down, four-three. Biff was on second. It was a situation where there was really no coaching strategy. Jerry either got a hit or made an out.

He had made hits in his three previous trips, but those were all in meaningless situations. I couldn't tell if he was setting us up to lose. Until that moment.

"Come on, Jerry," I yelled, clapping my hands. "I know you can do it."

If you *want* to, I silently added.

Jerry took two strikes over the heart of the plate. The bat never left his shoulder. All my secret little fantasies of an undefeated season were about to go up in smoke. I started mentally rehearsing my after-game speech, about how we gave it all we had, we'll get 'em next time, blah blah blah.

The beanpole on the mound kicked up his leg and brought the cheese. Jerry laced it off the fence in right-center. Dana waved Biff around to score, and Jerry was rounding second. I didn't know whether I hoped Dana would motion him to try for third, because Wheat Bran was due up next, and he'd yet to hit even a foul tip all season. But the issue was decided when their shortstop, the undertaker's kid, rifled the relay throw over the third basemen's head as Jerry pounded down the basepath. We won, five-four.

"I never doubted you guys for a second," I told the team afterward, but of course Jerry had already pulled his disappearing act.

Dana was blunt at dinner as I served up some tastiwhiz and fauxburger. I'd popped a cork on some decent wine to celebrate.

"Steve, I think you're beginning to like winning just a

little too much," she said, ever the concerned wife.

I grinned around a mouthful of food. "It gets in your blood," I said. "Can't help it."

"What about all those seasons you told the kids to just give it their best, back when you were plenty satisfied if everyone only showed a little improvement over the course of the season?"

"Back when I was just trying to build their self-esteem? Well, nothing builds character like winning. The little guys are practically *exploding* with character."

"I wish you were doing more for Jerry," she said. "He still doesn't act like part of the team. And the way he looks at you, like he wants you for a father figure. I think he's down on himself."

"Down on himself? *Down* on himself?" I almost sprayed my mouthful of wine across the table, and that stuff was ten bucks a bottle. I gulped and continued. "I could trade him for an entire *team* if I wanted. He's the best player to come out of Sawyer Creek since—"

"—since Roscoe Turnbull. And you see how *he* ended up."

I didn't like where this discussion was headed. "I'm sure Jerry's proud of his play. And the team likes him."

"Only because the team's winning. But I wonder how they would have reacted, how their *parents* would have reacted, if Jerry had struck out that last time today? I mean, nobody's exactly inviting him for sleep-overs as it is."

"He's just quiet. A lone wolf. Nothing wrong with that," I said, a little unsure of myself.

"Nothing wrong with vampires as long as they hit .921, is that what you mean?"

"Hey, we're winning, and that's what counts."

"I don't know," Dana said, shaking her pretty and sad head. "You're even starting to sound like Roscoe Turnbull."

That killed *my* mood, all right. That killed my mood for a lot of things around the house for a while. Lying in bed that night with a frigid three feet between us, I stared out the window at the full moon. A shape fluttered across it, a small lonely speck lost in that great circle of white. It most likely wasn't Jerry, but I felt an ache in my heart for him all the same.

At practice, I sometimes noticed the players whispering to each other while Jerry was at bat. I don't think for a minute that children are born evil. But they have parents who teach and guide them. Parents who were brought up on the same whispered myths.

I tried to be friendly toward Jerry, and kept turning my head so I could catch the look from him that Dana had described. But all I saw were a pair of bright eyes that could pierce the back of a person's skull if they wanted. Truth be told, he *did* give me the creeps, a little. And I could always pretend my philosophy was to show no favoritism, despite Dana's urging me to reach out to him.

Dana was a loyal assistant regardless of our difference of opinion. She helped co-pilot the Red Sox through the next eight victories. Jerry continued to tear up the league's pitching and played shortstop like a strip of flypaper, even though he was booed constantly. Elise pitched well and the rest of the kids were coming along, improving every game. I was almost sad when we got to the last game. I didn't want the season to end.

Naturally, we had to play the Turnbull Construction Claw Hammers for the championship. They'd gone undefeated in their division again. Ted had a fastball that could shatter a brick. And Roscoe Turnbull started scouting his draft picks while they were still in kindergarten, so he had the market cornered on talent.

I was so nervous I couldn't eat the day of the game. I got to the field early, while the caretaker was still trimming the outfield. Turnbull was there, too. He was in the home team's dugout shaving down a wooden bat. Wooden bats weren't even used in the majors anymore. Turnbull could afford lithium compound bats. That's when I first started getting suspicious.

"I'm looking forward to the big game," Turnbull said, showing the gaps between his front teeth.

"Me, too," I said, determined not to show that I cared. "And may the best team win."

"What do you mean? The best team always wins."

I didn't like the way he was running that woodshaver down the bat handle.

"You getting all nostalgic?" I asked, tremblingly nonchalant. "Going back to wood?"

"Good enough for my daddy. And my great-great-grandpaw on my mother's side. Maybe you heard of him. Tyrus Cobb."

The Hall-of-Famer. The Georgia Peach. The greatest hitter in any league, ever. Or the dirtiest player ever to set foot on a diamond, depending on whom you asked.

"Yeah, I've heard of him," I said. "That's quite a bloodline."

"Well, *we've* always managed to win without no lowdown, stinking vampires on our team."

"Jerry Shepherd deserves to play as much as any other boy or girl."

"It ain't right. Here this—" he made a spitting face— "*creature* has all these advantages like being able to change into an animal or throw the hocus-pocus on other players."

"You know that's against the rules. We'd be disqualified if he tried something like that. There's no advantage."

"It's only against the rules if you get caught." Turnbull held the tip of the bat up in the air. It was whittled to a fine, menacing point. "And sometimes, you got to *make* your advantages."

"Even you wouldn't stoop that low," I said. "Not just to win a game."

A thin stream of saliva shot from his mouth and landed on the infield dirt. He smiled again, the ugliest smile imaginable. "Gotta keep a little something on deck, just in case."

I shuddered and walked back to my dugout. Turnbull wasn't that bloodthirsty. He was just trying to gain a psychological edge. Sure, that was all.

Psychological edges work if you let them, so I spent the next fifteen minutes picking rocks from the infield. The kids were starting to arrive by then, so I watched them warm up. Jerry was late, as usual, but he walked out of the woods just as I was writing his name into the lineup. I nodded at him without speaking.

We batted first. Ted was starting for the Claw Hammers, of course. He was the kind of pitcher who would throw a brushback pitch at his own grandmother, if he thought she were digging in on him. He stood on the mound and practiced his battle glare, then whipped the ball into the catcher's mitt. I had to admit, the goon sure knew how to bring it to the plate.

Half the town had turned out. The championship game always drew better than the town elections. Dana patted me on the back. She wasn't one to hold a grudge when times were tough.

"Play ball," the umpire shouted, and we did.

Elise strode confidently to the plate.

"Go after her, Tedder," Turnbull shouted through his cupped hands from the other dugout. "You can do it, big guy."

The first pitch missed her helmet by three inches. She dusted herself off and stood deeper in the batter's box. The next pitch made her dance. Ball two. But she was getting a little shaky. No one likes being used for target practice. The next pitch hit her bat as she ducked away. Foul, strike one.

Elise was trembling now. I hated the strategy they were using, but unfortunately it was working. The umpire didn't say a word.

"Attaboy," Turnbull yelled. "Now go in for the kill."

Ted whizzed two more strikes past her while she was still off-balance. Biff grounded out weakly to second. Jerry went up to the plate and dug in. Ted's next offering hit Jerry flush in the face.

Jerry went down like a shot. I ran up to him and knelt in the dirt, expecting to see broken teeth and blood and worse. But Jerry's eyes snapped open. Another myth about vampires is that they don't feel pain. There are other kinds of pain besides the physical, though, and I saw them in Jerry's red irises. He could hear the crowd cheering as clearly as I could.

"Kill the vampire," one parent said.

"Stick a stake in him," another shouted.

"The Unnatural strikes again," a woman yelled.

I looked into the home team's dugout and saw Turnbull beaming as if he'd just won a trip to Alpha Centauri.

I helped Jerry up and he jogged to first base. I could see a flush of pink on the back of the usually-pale neck. I wondered whether the color was due to rage or embarrassment. I had Dana give him the "steal" sign, but the redhead popped up to the catcher on the next pitch.

We held them scoreless in their half, despite Ted's getting a triple. My heart was pounding like a kid's toy drum on Xmas Day, but I couldn't let the players know I cared one way or the other. When we got that third out, I calmly gave the kids high fives as they came off the field. Sure, this was just another game like the Mona Lisa was just another painting.

So it went for another couple of innings, with no runners getting past second. Jerry got beaned on the helmet his next trip up. The crowd was cheering like mad as he fell. I looked out at the mob sitting in the bleachers, and the scariest thing was that it wasn't just our opponent's fans who were applauding.

There was the sheriff, pumping her fist in the air. The mayor looked around secretively, checked the majority opinion, then added his jeers to the din. Biff's mother almost wriggled out of her tanktop, she was screaming so enthusiastically. A little old lady in the front row was bellowing death threats through her megaphone.

I protested the beaning to the umpire. He was a plump guy, his face melted by gravity. He looked like he'd umpired back before the days of protective masks and had taken a few foul tips to the nose.

"You've got to warn the pitcher against throwing at my players," I said.

"Can't hurt a vampire, so what's the point?" the umpire snarled, spitting brown juice towards my shoes. So that was how it was going to be.

"Then you should throw the pitcher out of the game because of poor sportsmanship."

"And I ought to throw *you* out for delay of game." He yanked the mask back over his face, which was a great improvement on his looks.

I squeezed Jerry's shoulder and looked him fully in the

eyes for the first time since I'd known him. Maybe I'd been afraid he would mesmerize me.

"Jerry, I'm going to put in a pinch-runner for you," I said. "It's not fair for you to put up with this kind of treatment."

I'd said the words that practically guaranteed losing the game, but I wasn't thinking about that then. The decision was made on instinct, and instinct is always truer and more revealing than a rationalizing mind. Later on, that thought gave me my only comfort.

I signaled Dana to send in a replacement. But Jerry's eyes blazed like hot embers and his face contorted into various animal faces: wolf, bat, tiger, wolverine, then settled back into its usual wan constitution.

"No," he said. "I'm staying in."

He jogged to first before I could stop him.

"Batter up," the umpire yelled.

I went into the dugout. Dana gave me a hug. There were tears in her eyes. Mine, too, though I made sure no one noticed.

Jerry stole second and then third. Wheat Bran was at the plate, waving his bat back and forth. I knew his eyes were closed. Two strikes, two outs. I was preparing to send the troops back out onto the field when Wheat Bran blooped a single down the line in right. Jerry scored standing up.

Elise shut out the Claw Hammers until the bottom of the sixth. She was getting tired. This was ulcer time, and I'd quit pretending not to care about winning. Sweat pooled under my arms and the band of my cap was soaked. I kept clapping my hands, but my throat was too tight to yell much encouragement.

Their first batter struck out. The second batter sent a

hard grounder to Jerry. I was mentally ringing up the second out when someone in the stands shouted, "Bite me, blood-breath!"

The ball bounced off Jerry's glove and went into the outfield. The runner made it to second. Jerry stared at the dirt.

"Shake it off, Jerry," I said, but my voice was lost in the chorus of spectators, who were calling my shortstop every ugly name you could think of. The next batter grounded out to first, advancing the runner to third.

Two outs, and you know the way these things always work. Big Ted Turnbull dug into the batter's box, gripping the sharpened wooden bat. But I wasn't going to let him hurt us. I did what you always do to a dangerous hitter with first base open: I took the bat out of his hands. I told Elise to walk him intentionally.

Roscoe Turnbull glared at me with death in his eyes, but I had to protect my shortstop and give us the best chance to win. Ted reached first base and called time out, then jogged over to his team's bench. Roscoe gave me a smile. That smile made my stomach squirm as if I'd swallowed a dozen large snakes.

Ted sat down and changed his shoes. I didn't understand until he walked back onto the infield. The bottom of his cleats were so thick that they resembled those shoes the disco dancers wore after disco made its fourth comeback. The shoes made Ted six inches taller. The worst part was that the spikes were made of wood.

I thought of Ted's ancestor, Ty Cobb, how Cobb was legendary for sliding into second with his spikes high. I rocketed off the bench.

"Time!" I screamed. "Time out!"

The umpire lifted his mask.

"What now?" he asked.

I pointed to the cleats. "Those are illegal."

"The rule book only bans *metal* cleats," he said. "Now, batter up."

"Second baseman takes the throw on a steal," I shouted as instruction to my fielders.

"No," Jerry shouted back. He pointed to the plate. "Left-handed batter."

Shortstop takes the throw when a lefty's up. The tradition of playing the percentages was as old as baseball itself. Even with the danger, I couldn't buck the lords of the game. Unwritten rules are sometimes the strongest.

I sat on the bench with my heart against my tonsils. The crowd was chanting, "Spike him, spike him, spike him," over and over. Dana sat beside me and held my hand, a strange mixture of accusation and empathy in her eyes.

"Maybe the next batter will pop up," she said. "There probably won't even *be* a play at second."

"Probably not."

She didn't say anything about testosterone or my stubborn devotion to the percentages. Or that Elise was getting weaker and we had no relief pitcher. Or that we had to nail the lid on this victory quick or it would slip away. I knew what Dana was thinking, though.

"I'd do it even if it was my own son out there," I muttered to her. I almost even believed it.

They tried a double-steal on the next pitch. It was a delayed steal, where the runner on third waits for the catcher to throw down to second, then tries for home. Not a great strategy for the game situation, but I had a feeling Turnbull had a lower purpose in mind.

Biff gunned a perfect strike to Jerry at second. The play

unfolded as if in slow motion. Ted was already leaning back, launching into his slide.

Please step away, Jerry, I was praying. The runner on third was halfway home. If Jerry didn't make the tag, we'd be tied and the Claw Hammers would have the momentum. But I didn't care. I'd gladly trade safe for safe.

Jerry didn't step away. His instincts were probably screaming at him to change into a bat and flutter above the danger, or to paralyze Ted in his tracks with a deep stare. Maybe he knew that would have caused us to forfeit the game and the championship. Or maybe he was just stubborn like me.

He gritted his teeth, his two sharp incisors hanging over his lip in concentration. Ted slid into the bag, wooden spikes high in the air. Jerry stooped into the cloud of dust. He applied the tag just before the spikes caught him flush in the chest.

The field umpire reflexively threw his thumb back over his shoulder to signal the third out. But all I could see through my blurry eyes was Jerry writhing in the dirt, his teammates hustling to gather around him. I ran out to my vampire shortstop, kneeling beside his body just as the smoke started to rise from his flesh.

He gazed up at me, the pain dousing the fire in his eyes. The crowd was silent, hushed by the horror of a wish come true. The Red Sox solemnly removed their hats. I'd never heard such a joyless championship celebration. Jerry looked at me and smiled, even as his features dissolved around his lips.

"We won, Coach," he whispered, and that word "we" was like a stake in my own heart. Then Jerry was dust, forever part of the infield.

Dana took the pitcher's mound, weeping without shame. She stared into the crowd, at the umpires, into Turnbull's dugout, and I knew she was meeting the eye of every single person at Sawyer Field that day.

"Look at yourselves," she said, her voice strong despite the knots I knew were tied in her chest. "Just take a good long look."

Everybody did. I could hear a hot dog wrapper blowing against the backstop.

"All he wanted was to play," she said. "All he wanted was to be just like you."

Sure, her words were for everybody. But she had twenty-two years of experience as Mrs. Ruttlemyer. We both knew whom she was really talking to.

"Just like you," she whispered, her words barely squeezing out yet somehow filling the outfield, the sky, the little place in your heart where you like to hide bad things. She walked off the mound with her head down, like a pitcher that had just given up the game-winning hit.

So many tears were shed that the field would have been unplayable. People had tasted the wormwood of their prejudice. They had seen how vicious the human animal could be. Even vampires didn't kill their young, even when the young were decades old.

There was no memorial service. I wrote the eulogy, but nobody ever got to read it, not even Dana. There was talk of filing criminal charges against the Turnbulls, but nobody had the stomach to carry it through. What happened that day was something that people spent a lot of time trying to forget.

But that victory rang out across the ensuing years, a Liberty Bell for the living dead in Sawyer Creek. Vampires were embraced by the community, welcomed into the Chamber of Commerce, one was even elected mayor. Roscoe Turnbull has three vampires on his team this season.

That Sawyer Cup still sits on my mantel, even though I never set foot on a diamond after that day. Sometimes when I look at the trophy, I imagine it is full of blood. They say that winning takes sacrifice. But that's just a myth.

Still, all myths contain a kernel of truth, and even a myth can make you shiver.

Skin

Cold.

But that was wrong.

Should have been hot.

Fire lick orange. That was the last thing Roger remembered, until now.

Along with the chill, other sensations seeped into the murky pool of his thoughts.

Pain. A sheet of razors and barbed wire across his chest, an iron maiden mask closed on his face, sixty volts of electricity running through the fluids in his veins. Ground glass in his trachea when he tried to breath. Behind his eyelids, jagged lime and lemon shapes slicing at the jelly of his eyeballs.

"Moo fwing okay?" Words from somewhere above his seething cauldron of agony, muffled by what? The upholstery of his coffin? The idea of being dead made Roger panic, and he tried to open his eyes. A wedge of brightness cut across his vision like a saber. Tears welled, and the salt made his face erupt in fresh hurt.

A moist cloth descended and wiped softly at his eyelids. Cold. He shivered.

"Welcome back." A shape now, fuzzy, large, pale. Over him. He blinked twice and saw her. A woman in white, her face an oval blur.

Roger started to ask her where, what, why. But he could only gurgle weakly. There was a tube in his throat. He tried to push his tongue out to his lips, but the meat in his mouth was swollen.

"Take it easy, Mr. Fremont. You're going to be just fine." The words were as soothing as a vanilla milkshake.

Nurse. She was a nurse, not Grandma Cuvier. So he wasn't dead after all. He felt a draft, saw another shape join the first. Another woman, this one wearing a drab turquoise apron.

"He's awake," said the first. The new arrival bent over him. She wrinkled her nose at the scent of his cooked flesh.

"Hello, Mr. Fremont," she said, and her words were frosty, clotted, like a daiquiri. "I'm Dr. Ghalani. You're a very lucky man, though you might not think so at the moment. But we'll have you back on your feet in no time."

He tried to speak again, and this time managed a grunt.

"Save your strength. Burns take a long time to heal, so the best thing for you to do is learn how to be patient."

Patient. Burns. Doctor. The fire.

"I'm sorry we can't give you any painkillers," said the female voice. "Unfortunately, the systemic injuries are so severe that we can't risk burdening your respiratory system. But maybe in a day or two..."

Day or two? How long had he been lying under this sharp sheet? That meant somebody else was running the restaurant, probably skimming money from the register. Or else the insurance company was ripping him off by finding some obscure clause in his fire coverage.

Roger tried to raise himself off the bed. His body was a water balloon. The effort undulated uselessly down to his lower limbs, awakening dormant nerve endings. The waves rebounded and raced to his brain, carrying fishhooks and shark's teeth and sharp broken coral in on the tide. This time his throat and tongue worked, but the scream was gargled and weak.

"Don't try to move," Dr. Ghalani said. "You'll heal faster if you stay still and let your body do its work."

Roger wept again, but this time no wet cloth came to his rescue. He didn't trust women. Grandma Cuvier said they were leeches, wanting only blood and money. And a woman doctor was the worst of all.

Dr. Ghalani turned to the nurse. "It's time for another scraping, then we can change his bandages."

Roger heard a sound that was unmistakable to someone who had cooked for fourteen years: the rattle of cutlery on stainless steel. He felt a tug on his abdomen, and a liquid tearing noise reached his ears a split second before the pain hit. Sparks of fluorescent custard yellow and vivid red jumped the wires in his brain. They were flaying him.

He tried to turn his head, to scream, to run, but he was beached, bloated. He saw another shape in the corner, and his last thought was that the medical team had called in an extra hand to help shred his flesh from his bones. Then he passed out.

The fire.

He should have known better than to throw water on a grease fire. But the grill and deep fryers and stoves were all fueled by propane. If the fire reached the tank...

Explosion.

His eyes snapped open. The dull greenish striplights above stared back without pity. How long? He shifted his gaze to the window. Black, so it must be night.

The shape in the corner. A doctor? Nurse? Roger tried to call out, but his vocal chords were still knotted.

The shape moved. Was he injured so badly that he required constant supervision? This was going to cost him a bundle. Grandma Cuvier said that modern medicine was just highway robbery without the highway. Chicken blood and bone powder and a little prayer were the best cures.

He shivered, his body icy. That didn't make sense. How could you be cold when you were burned? And why did his body feel so thick? He'd always been lean, despite the lure of an endless supply of available food. Now the thought of food sliding down his raw throat almost made him want to vomit, and if he vomited when he couldn't turn his head, he might choke. Even if his stomach were empty, just the convulsions jarring his body would be a hellish torture.

He wished the shadow-person would come to his bedside and murmur some placating words. Even if they were lies. He wouldn't mind having his eyelids wiped. And now that he was fully awake, he became aware of the itch.

Not just a single itch. A thousand feathertips were at his flesh, tickling, quivering, probing. He was lying on straw. He was dressed in burlap, with fiberglass insulation stuffed down his collar and cuffs.

He wished the person would scratch him, plow his skin with a weedrake. He managed a groan, hoping the noise would bring the caregiver closer. No luck. What kind of hospital were they running here? No painkillers, no attention, and probably a hefty daily charge for all the needles and tubes that were jabbed into his body.

Itching. Waiting. The night didn't move. Neither did the shadow-shape.

He thought of the years he'd spent working his way from dishwasher to restaurant owner, how everybody had wanted a piece of him, a handout. Well, he only wanted what was his. And the hospital officials and the insurance company were probably working together to make sure they took everything from him. The anger added to his discomfort and kept him from sleeping.

After what seemed to be years, the window grayed, then brightened. Morning. The corner where the shadow had been was now empty. Dr. Ghalani came into the room.

"And how are we today, Mr. Fremont?" She sounded like a bird, cheery, happy. She wasn't the one who was suspended in sawdust and wool and nails and shrapnel. He wheezed a complaint.

"Don't try to speak." She looked at the machines above the bed, wrote some numbers on a clipboard. "Your blood pressure is up. You're on the mend."

She peeled back what felt like a carpet's-thickness of Roger's flesh, though surely it was only the gauze she was lifting. He squeaked like a rat caught in a trap.

"Looks like the graft is taking." The doctor sounded pleased with herself.

Graft? She must have seen his eyes widen.

"Skin graft. To allow your own skin a chance to grow back. You might feel a little itching, but it's only natural."

Roger guessed she'd never been a burn victim herself. There was nothing natural about his "little itching." What did she care? She was getting paid the same whether he lived or died.

He licked his lips and felt ragged tissue. There were

bandages on his face. How much of him was burned? Did he have eyebrows?

Was his face damaged? He hadn't been the most handsome guy around, but he'd grown accustomed to the slab of skin and cartilage that had stared back at him from the mirror all his life. And what was a guy besides his face?

It figured. Grandma had warned that the world was out to get them. He'd developed a tough hide, but maybe not tough enough.

A moan rose from his heavy chest. Dr. Ghalani patted him gently on a part of his body that must have been his arm. She didn't wipe his tears. "Don't worry. We'll have you good as new before you know it."

Someone else came in the room. A nurse, different from the first one. "His respiration and EKG are strong enough now that we can give him some morphine in his drip," Dr. Ghalani said to the nurse. Dr. Ghalani was reeling off some dosage instructions, but Roger had shifted his attention across the room, to the shadow in the corner.

It wasn't medical personnel. The shadow wasn't wearing white. The shadow was red, the color of a peeled tomato. A visitor? Why would anyone visit him, unless it was to borrow money or steal his wallet?

Grandma Cuvier would visit him, to mumble prayers and rub potions on his feet. But she was dead. The only person he could ever trust. The only person who hadn't wanted a piece of him.

He tried to focus on the visitor, but his vision blurred. Then he was soaring in ice water, swimming in blue sky, swelling like a summer cloud, riding a rainbow sled into unconsciousness.

The tube was gone from Roger's mouth when he awoke. The window was black, meaning he'd slept through the day. The pain was nothing but a dull steady throb, like the itching, both merely background noise to his buzzing brain. He could move his arms a little under the sheet. They felt like sausages.

Roger raised his head and looked in the corner. The red shadowy visitor was there, standing. Probably a claims agent from the insurance company, come to give him the shaft while he was too weak to fight back. Roger tried his voice.

"Heeeey," he wheezed. His lungs raged with the effort of drawing air. The red shadow shifted a step closer, almost into the full glare of the fluorescent lights. The door to the room swiveled open, blocking Roger's view of the shadow.

The nurse came in, the one who had spoken to him when he first regained consciousness in the hospital. He remembered how she had wiped around his eyes with the damp cloth. He tried to smile at her, then realized that he probably had no lips.

"Well, hello, Mr. Fremont," she said. "I hear you're coming along just fine."

"Huh...hello," he whispered.

"So we're talking now. That's wonderful." She checked the machines. Roger smelled her perfume, and it was a pleasant change from the days or weeks of smelling his own barbecued flesh and the burn ointments. Then he remembered the visitor in the corner.

"The vultures can't...wait," he said. His throat was dry but he was overjoyed to be able to make words again. Now he could tell those doctors and lawyers and crooks what he thought of them.

"Sutures? They'll be out soon."

She'd misunderstood. He tried to raise his hand and

point, but she lightly touched his arm. "Now, now, mustn't stretch the grafts, Mr. Fremont. The new skin is still trying to make itself at home."

Home. He'd read about how they took skin from a different area of a person's body for transplants during plastic surgery or burn treatment. But he didn't have enough healthy skin left to provide his own. His entire upper body was encased in bandages, along with his face. They'd probably given him the most costly treatment ever invented.

"Swollen." He had trouble enunciating the labials.

"It's your body's way of fighting off infection. Your immune system is sending plasma and antibodies to the injured areas. Nothing to worry about." She lifted a bandage from his chest and peered at the burns.

"Nu— 'nother nurse?" He rolled his eyes to the place where the shadow had been.

"No, there's not another nurse. I'm afraid you're stuck with little old me tonight." She checked his drip, and Roger felt the first stirrings of disorientation. "Rest easy now," she said, walking toward the door.

Roger wanted to call her back, to tell her not to go, he itched, he was in pain, anything to make her stay. But already his tongue felt thick and alien in his mouth, as if he were sucking on cotton. The door swung closed.

The red shadow was silent in the corner. It stepped forward. Roger was glad he still had eyelids. He clamped them down and tried to remember how to pray. He thought of Grandma Cuvier, how she knelt beside his bed when he was young, clutching her beads and crosses in her gnarled fingers. What were her words?

He almost remembered by the time he finally fell asleep.

"You're much improved, Roger," Dr. Ghalani said. She was calling him by his first name now. To Roger, that was a sign that he'd been in the hospital far too long.

"The burns," he said. "How bad?"

"Unfortunately, some were third degree, meaning the damage reached the fat and muscle. Other areas weren't as severely affected."

Roger could raise his bandaged arms now. He looked like a mummy in an old Universal movie, one of the goofy ones with Abbott and Costello. The skin under the wraps was trying to merge with his meat. He had to know.

"Where...the skin for the grafts." Needles and razors were in his throat. "Whose was it?"

"Donor skin. Ideally, we would use your own skin, but in this case, the injuries were too widespread."

"Donor?"

Dr. Ghalani pursed her thin lips as if coming to a decision. "Taken from cadavers."

So he was inside another person's skin. The person who was standing in the corner, the wet shadow, the thing that was watching with bright wide eyes.

Because he remembered one of Grandma Cuvier's stories. About how a person couldn't get into heaven unless they had all their body parts, because God wanted His angels to come inside the Pearly Gates all beautiful and whole and perfect. And those that lost a part were doomed to walk the earth until they were able to reunite their bodies and thus their souls.

Dr. Ghalani must have seen the fear light his eyes. "It's perfectly safe. The skin is tested for infectious diseases before being removed. It protects your body until your own epidermal layers have a chance to rebuild themselves."

Roger trembled under his sheet.

"Cold? Your regulatory system is still trying to regain its ability to control body temperature. I'll have the nurse turn up the thermostat." She gave a professional smile. "I believe you're scheduled to begin your physical rehabilitation today. I'll bet you're looking forward to getting out of that bed for a while."

Roger gulped some sharp air and looked at the red thing in the corner. No, it wasn't in the corner anymore. It was closer, near enough for Roger to see the gleam of its teeth against the pink of the gums. Its eyes were naked glass. The lack of lips gave the thing a gleeful grin.

"I've got to finish my rounds, Roger," the doctor said. "See you later."

She whirled and stood face-to-face with the red shadow. She didn't scream. She walked through it and out the door.

The thing drifted closer. Roger could smell it now, a decaying corruption mingled with the coppery odor of blood. Stipples of red fluid stood out from the bands of gristle.

"Go away," Roger whispered. Grandma's stories were just old folk tales. Ghosts weren't real. "You're not real."

The red corpse's grin deepened. It was ten feet away now.

The door swiveled open. A short man with muscular hairy arms came in the room. "Hi, Roger. Ready to get back on your feet?"

Roger was more than ready. He wanted to regain the ability to run.

"We'll take it slow today," the therapist said. "Maybe get you down for a workout by the end of the week."

The corpse watched as the man eased Roger out of bed. Roger watched back. As the therapist waltzed Roger and worked his limbs, Roger had the feeling that the corpse also wanted a spot on his dance card.

Night came, as always, too soon. The ward was quiet, not even the squeak of stretcher wheels in the hallway outside. The red thing had maintained its vigil. Now it sat in a chair beside Roger's bed. Sweat moistened Roger's bandages in the places where the skin was undamaged enough to exude liquid.

Roger felt much better. He had a new theory, one that made more sense than Grandma's strange beliefs. It was the drugs doing it, making him have hallucinations. Good, expensive drugs.

A low-voltage shock of worry tingled in the back of his mind, about how the corpse had appeared before the drugs were administered. But that period was hazy, just a long agonizing fog. Pain was probably just as much of a mental trickster as drugs. Sure, that was it. He might as well amuse himself, to help pass the time.

"H—hello," Roger said. The corpse only slumped lower in the chair.

Strips of tendon and muscle stretched over the red thing's skeletal frame. The corpse wasn't entirely skinned: it looked as if it were wearing gloves. As if whoever had performed the butchery avoided the areas that were too troublesome to peel.

"I know why you're here," Roger said. The corpse grinned wetly, showing too many teeth.

"I'm sorry about what they did," Roger said. He tried to roll over, but his body was too weak to respond. Dr. Ghalani said he was getting better. Then why was he so tired?

"It was on me when I regained consciousness." Roger was pleading now, whining. The raw face with its too-wide eyes leaned closer. One of the skin-gloved hands reached out to Roger's chest.

Roger tried to duck away, but the metal rails kept him imprisoned in the bed. He screamed, but no sound came from his throat. Only a bad dream, he told himself. Only a bad dream. That's why the scream didn't bring hospital staff running.

The hand was on him now, its fingernails probing into the moist bandages. The funk of rot mingled with the smell of salve. The cold hand was now in contact with Roger's chest, Roger's skin.

No, not *my* skin, Roger thought. *His* skin.

A rattle of cutlery.

There was no pain as the blade sliced into the flesh. Roger heard the scraping noises even over the pounding of his heart in his ears. The scalpel slid lower, across Roger's stomach, the thing's other hand scooping and clawing as it followed the instrument. Then the hand went up, around the sides, to the edges of the healthy skin.

Roger tried to scream again, but his mouth was cloth, his tongue cotton. He closed his eyes, but the snick-snick of the flaying only grew louder. And the fingers were on his neck. The blade raked a seam up to Roger's chin, then to his mouth.

Roger looked at the red thing's eyes. They were lifeless, without pity, but a grim determination shone in the tiny pupils. The hand worked its way along his cheek. Silver flashed as the blade scraped up to his temples and across his forehead.

Roger tensed as the instrument stroked near his eyes. If the thing wanted revenge, it could choose a hundred places. His face, his exposed lips, his ears. Claim a scalp. Or down below, things at lower regions.

But the corpse only peeled up to the beginning of Roger's hairline, to the point where the skin grafts stopped. Then Roger knew. It wanted its skin back. Skin that it needed before it could move on to the next plane, to heaven or hell or wherever else that wholeness was required.

Roger brought his own bandaged hands up and feverishly raked at his chest and neck, heedless of the pain as he peeled and clawed at the foreign matter clinging to his body. He grunted as he shed himself of the invading skin that clung to his own newly-grown cells. He wanted nothing that belonged to a dead person. He wanted freedom, just as this walking nightmare sought its own release.

A long minute's clumsy rending, and the work was done. The dead thing gathered the loose skin in its arms and stepped away from Roger's bed. It stood for a moment under the fluorescent lights, its gleaming flesh in contrast to the pile of pale material clasped to its chest. Its eyes met Roger's, and there was no relief or gratitude in them. Nothing.

As it turned and shuffled back into the shadows, Roger realized that the naked corpse had recovered only a portion of its skin, that it still wasn't dressed for the afterlife. It would have to make other stops.

Roger closed his eyes and tried to remember how to pray.

"Very good." Dr. Ghalani put the bandages back in place. Another doctor stood beside her, tall and with a thick mustache. He looked and smelled expensive. Two doctors for the price of three, probably.

"Good?" Roger thought she would notice that the skin grafts were gone.

"Yes. Your own skin is growing back. The graft is sloughing off."

"Sloughing?"

"The body always rejects foreign skin. It's only a temporary cover to give you time to heal."

Foreign skin. If that was good news, why wasn't she smiling? Did the insurance bills not clear?

"How are you feeling?" she asked.

"Fine." Much better, now that the corpse was gone. Now that he had only his own skin to worry about. "Except I'm a little tired."

Dr. Ghalani frowned. "Yes. Something showed up in your tests."

"Tests?"

"The metabolic strain from the burns. Your regulatory system was severely damaged. We've moved fast on this. You're luckier than most."

Roger tried to swallow, but felt as if a pill the size of a football was lodged in his throat.

"I'm afraid there's been permanent liver damage."

Roger looked from Dr. Ghalani to the new doctor.

"This is Dr. Wood," she said. "He's here to talk to you about your transplant."

Roger's scream awoke a donor's gutted corpse six hundred miles away.

Dead Air

I leaned back in my swivel chair, my headphones vice-gripping my neck. The VU meters were pinned in the red, and Aerosmith had the monitor speakers throbbing. I turned down the studio sound level and pressed the phone to my ear, not believing what I'd heard.

"I've just killed a man," she repeated, her voice harsh and breathless.

"Come again, sister?" I said, pulling my feet off the console. My brain was a little slow in catching on. I was two hours into the graveyard shift, and the before-work beers were crashing into my third cup of cold coffee like Amtrak trains.

"I've just killed a man," she said for a third time. She was a little calmer now. "I just wanted to share that with you. Because I've always felt like I could trust you. You have an honest voice."

I potted up the telephone interface and broadcast her live to my loyal listeners. All three of them, I chuckled to myself. In five years at WKIK, The Kick, I'd come to accept my humble place in the universe. The only people tuned in at this hour were hepped-up truckers and vampire wannabes, the unwashed who shied from the light of day. I'd long ago decided that I might as well keep myself amused. And now I had a nutter on the line.

I flipped my mic key and the red "ON AIR" sign blinked over the door.

"Yo, this is Mickey Nixon with ya in the wee hours," I said, in the slightly-false bass I'd cultivated over the course of my career. "I've got a talker on the line, she's there to share. Go on, honey."

"I just want everybody to know that I killed someone. This man I've been dating got a little bit too aggressive, so I blew his damned brains out. And it felt good," she said, her words pouring out over the monitors through the warm Kansas air.

My finger was poised over the mute button in case I needed to censor her. By station rules, I was supposed to send all live call-ins through the loop delay. But since I got so few callers, I usually took my chances. Plus I liked the razor edge of spontaneity.

"I want to tell you that the steam off his blood is still rising. He's lying here on his apartment floor with his pants around his knees and his brains soaking into the shag carpet. If any of you guys out there think date rape is a laughing matter, I'm sharing this little story so you'll think twice."

I gulped. This was really wacky stuff. I couldn't have written it in a million years. I'd paid friends before to call with outrageous stories, but they always sounded a little too rehearsed. Now here was some dynamite, and it was exploding at no charge.

"Wait a minute, woman," I said, playing the straight man. "You mean to tell us you're standing over a warm body right now with a phone in your hand, confessing murder?"

"It's not murder, it's self-defense. I may be a woman, but I've got my rights. Nobody touches me unless I let them. Besides, I've done this before, I've just never felt like talking about it until now."

"So maybe it's what you would call a 'justifiable' homicide. Have you called the police?"

I was starting to get a little nervous now. If this girl was acting, she was too good to be stuck in a Midwestern cow town like Topeka. She was starting to sound too weird, even for me. Her voice was as sharp and cold as an icicle, but with a touch of sexiness all the same.

"That's why I called you, Mickey. I've listened to your show for a long time, and I just knew you'd understand. You think the boys in blue would believe me?"

I was almost flattered, but a reality check rose like stomach acid. Sure, years ago I was a morning star in Los Angeles drive-time, but a little FCC controversy knocked me down faster than a Mike Tyson punch. I'd bounced around a few AM stations and tried my hand at ad sales, but now I was just riding the board until the years of chemical abuse caught up with me.

"Honey, I'm here for you," I said, getting back in the game. "We love you here at the Kick, and Mickey Nixon is not one to judge other people. Live and let live, I always say...to coin a phrase."

Now I could see a row of green lights blinking on the telephone board. Four callers were waiting to be punched in. I'd never had more than two, and that was when Lefty from Promotions had fingered me a couple of White Zombie tickets to give away. This girl, whoever she was, had the audience stirring.

"Mickey, men have always disappointed me. They talk sweet and walk straight until they get what they want. Then they treat you like a rag doll or worse. Well, I'm fed up. Now, I'm the one on the prowl for easy meat. Just ask Chuck here..."

There were a couple of seconds of dead air.

"Oh, sorry. Chucky can't come to the phone right now. He's got other things on his mind, and they're called my feet. Well, Mickey. I've got to go. It's been real, and I'll be in touch."

I could hear sirens in the background just before she hung up.

"If you're still out there, remember that you can talk to me. I'll never do you wrong," I broadcast to the sleepy world. I punched up caller number two, trying to keep some momentum.

"Hey, Mickey, that tart's gone out of her mind. Did you pay a friend of yours to call in or something?" a drunken voice slurred.

"Yeah, just like I did with you, upchuck breath." I cut him off and punched up the next caller.

"I just killed a beer myself, and I want you to know your show rocks, man."

It sounded like a college student who had seen "Wayne's World" too many times. But I wasn't choosy and I doubted I'd be lucky enough to get anyone as interesting as my death-dealing diva as an on-air guest. What was I expecting, Howard Stern or the ghost of Orson Welles?

"That chick was really wild, man," the caller continued, adding a couple of "uhs" into the mix. This show was billed as the "Talk-n-Toonage Marathon," but the talk never seemed to keep rolling.

"Thanks for the input, 'dude.' Gotta go." I sighed, stabbed the button on the cart machine, and AC/DC started ringing "Hell's Bells."

The next afternoon, I rolled out of bed and belched stale coffee. I stumbled through the dirty clothes and back issues of *Rolling Stone* that served as the carpet in my one-room bachelor's paradise and elbowed open the bathroom door. I showered and even screwed up my resolve enough to shave. I felt displaced and alienated, as if I'd just come back from a long drug trip. At first, I couldn't figure out what was different. Then it hit me. I actually felt rejuvenated, as if last night's caller had given me something to look forward to.

I drove my ragged Honda down to the station and parked at the far end of the lot. All the other jocks had personal spaces. I guess the station GM figured one day I'd just disappear and she didn't want me around badly enough to invest ten bucks in a lousy plywood sign. Well, no love lost.

I went inside and checked the shift schedule, then headed for the staff lounge. I was just about to scarf a couple of donuts when I saw the newspaper open on the table. I picked it up and searched the front page. No headlines screaming bloody murder.

I was turning to the crime section when Pudge, WKIK's answer to Benito Mussolini as well as Program Director, walked in. His eyes glared from under the caterpillars of his brows. He didn't bother saying hello. He had a marketing report in his hand and he waved it like an ax.

"Your numbers are down, Mick. You know the only reason we stay on during the graveyard shift is because it's cheaper than locking up and paying security for a few hours. But I want to lead in every time slot, and you're not up to speed."

Pudge was on a mission to inflate his own ego until his

head could no longer fit through doorways. He gobbled up credit like it was free pizza, but when it was time to dish out the blame, he had a list as long as his belt, and his name was on the last notch. College communications courses taught me that radio was a personal medium, but Pudge must have skipped those. At every staff meeting, he argued for total automation of WKIK.

I rubbed my cheek and felt the first blossom of stubble in the weedbeds of my cheeks.

"Well, Pu— um, Andrew, if you'd give my slot a little promotion, it might do something. Besides, I've got a loyal audience."

"Well, your audience's demographic doesn't coincide with the one our advertisers want to reach. Even at your low wage, this 'Talk-n-Toonage Marathon' is barely breaking even. I'm tempted to change your slot to a satellite feed."

I was barely listening because I was transfixed by the flapping of his plump lips. He bored me faster than a dinner date with Andre. I muttered something appropriately offensive and incoherent and left with the newspaper and a pair of chocolate donuts. The Honda whined a little before starting, but I coaxed it home so that I could rest before the night's shift.

As I gnawed a three-day-old slice of anchovy pizza, I thumbed through the paper. On page two of the local news section, I found my item.

MAN FOUND DEAD IN
APPARENT HOMICIDE

Charles Shroeder, age 29, of 417 Skylark Place, was found shot in his home last night. Police responded after a neighbor reported hearing a gunshot. A medical examiner ruled that

Shroeder died from a single bullet wound to the head at approximately 2:00 AM. There are no suspects at this time, according to Lt. C.L. Hubble of the Topeka Police Detective Division.

So my mystery caller was the real thing after all. I wondered if I should call the police. I didn't have any solid evidence, if you didn't count a phone conversation, and I didn't. I decided to wait until she called again. I wanted to hear her voice, the one of blood and smoke. I only hoped she wouldn't have to kill again, if indeed she had killed at all, to be motivated enough to give me a ring.

Four long, lonely nights crawled by. "Wayne" called once and requested some Beastie Boys, and a handful of callers asked about the "murder woman," but other than that, the phone set in its cradle like a cement slipper. I slid into my regular routine, ignoring the playlist and forgetting to air the paid ads according to the traffic schedule. My cynicism began to consume me again, a snake swallowing its tail. Then, on Thursday, she called.

I knew it was her the moment I saw the light on the switchboard. I snapped the phone to my ear. "Mickey Nixon at the Kick."

"Hi, Mickey. It's me again." Her voice rushed through the miles of cable like a May breeze, warm and fresh.

"You have me at a disadvantage. I don't know your name."

"That would sort of be like kissing and telling, wouldn't it? You already know so much about me. But just call me 'Night Owl.'"

I eyed the digits counting down on the Denon player and cued the next CD. So she'd given herself a pseudonym.

Not exactly a sign of emotional stability. But, hell, my real name was Michel D'artagne.

"Well, do you want to tell our audience what you've been doing with yourself lately?"

"Anything for a thrill, Mickey. Have you missed me?"

"Sure. It's a lonely life, surrounded by these cold machines. The music helps, but it's the people that make it matter. I'm sending you out live now." I potted up the interface before beginning my introduction.

"Yo, shake out of those dreams, my friend, Mickey's got the Night Owl here, the one that's to die for, and you want to twist that dial right on up."

Deejaying was one of the few occupations where you could get away with referring to yourself in the third person, along with politics and professional sports. She picked up on my enthusiasm and jumped right in.

"Hey, out there in radio-land. This is Night Owl with more good news for the human race. There's one less piece of dirtbaggage in the world tonight. I just took down number three. Johnny picked me up in a bar and wanted a double-handful of hot romance. He got an earful of hot metal instead. Just because he bought me a drink, he thought he was buying the whole package."

I could see the switchboard lighting up like a Christmas tree. WKIK's phone system could handle eight lines, and every one had a caller on the end. Apparently, word had trickled out like electricity. I'd been searching my whole career for something to strike the audience's nerves, and it seemed death did the trick.

"Night Owl, some of our audience would like to talk to you. Go ahead, caller one..." I potted up our auxiliary phone link so we could have a three-way conversation.

"Thank you for bringing joy to my life," a woman's cigarette-scorched voice came over the monitors. "I've been married to a slob for eighteen years, and suddenly he's turned into Mr. Clean, minus the earring. He heard about you down at the Pump-And-Pay, and he figured he'd better get his act together, because you never know who's going to turn into a copycat killer. Keep up the good work, girl."

I punched up another. It was Wayne, my main man. Maybe he had something bright to say for once. He stuttered a couple of times before starting. "Hey, Miss Night Owl lady, I dig your style. I know us men can be, like, pigs and stuff, but don't you think killing's a little harsh?"

"Desperate times call for desperate measures," Night Owl said. "I think thousands of years of male-dominated society are enough, don't you?"

"Well, uh—" Wayne was at a loss for words. Maybe he'd used up the dozen he knew. But he coughed and continued. "I guess there's some bad guys, but it's not, you know, a total washout with us dude-types."

"Oh, there are a few good men, and believe me, they're not in the Marines. Take our Mickey, for instance."

"Thanks, Night Owl." I was beginning to wonder if I knew this woman. I'd always had a soft spot for sweet psychos. "Do you have time for another caller?"

Wayne cut in like a cowboy at a line dance. "Would you like to, like, go out or something, Night Owl?"

"Well, you definitely sound like my type. My type of victim, that is. Who knows, maybe we'll meet. I'll keep one in the chamber, just for you."

I punched up another caller. It was a woman.

"I'm right with you, honey. I dated a clown for seven years, and ever doggone time I brought up marriage, he'd say,

'Why buy the cow when you can get the milk for free?' Well, I put a good dose of digitalis in a cherry cheesecake— do you bake? I got some good recipes. Been in the family for generations— well, the idiot ate it. He was grinnin' like a turtle eatin' saw-briars the whole time. Fell over dead right there at the kitchen table. Had a weak heart, I told the police. Well, I may be the cow, but he's the one who kicked the bucket. And I got you to thank for gettin' up my nerve."

"Another blow for freedom, my dear," Night Owl said. "Keep that oven warm. Sounds like you're a real killer cook. Well, folks, gotta run. There's nothing I hate worse than being a cold-blooded murderer, so I try to leave before rigor mortis sets in. Bye, Mickey, smooches to you."

As she hung up, I felt like I was in a vacuum. I was annoyed by my attraction to her. I was beginning to understand the audience's fascination with Night Owl. I punched up another caller.

We filled the air of the black Kansas sky with talk about the Equal Rights Amendment, the best methods of undetected murder, and even shared a few culinary tips. The switchboard stayed full most of the shift. I slipped in a few hard rock tunes and a couple of ads without losing talkers. The night flowed by like warm honey.

By the time the sun was stabbing over the flat horizon, I was wrapping up the best shift I'd ever had. Reluctantly. I turned the board over to Georgie Boy, host of the Kick's Morning Show. I signed off on the transmitter log and went home. I was so wired, I didn't fall asleep until noon. A lot of people probably called in sick that morning.

Night Owl didn't phone the next week, but plenty of others did. Some were women confessing murder. A few guys apologized for the whole male gender. Most people quite simply wanted to talk about death and dying, especially of the "unnatural" variety.

I played the role of arbitrator. I'd never fought in the battle of the sexes, so I just stood by and counted casualties. I changed the name of the show to "Death Radio," and I even had some celebrities dialing in. I was caught in the flush of excitement. I felt free, like a teenager with his first car and the whole bright future laid out in front of him like a six-lane highway.

There was a rash of homicides in the city, and officials had no explanation. Gun sales were up, but robbery and rape were way down. My show was number one with a bullet among the overnights in my market. When I went to pick up my check one Friday, I ran into Pudge. He looked like a cat that had swallowed curdled cream.

"Congratulations, Mick. In three weeks, you've escalated to the top of your time slot. We've got sponsors lining up to take your show. We can pretty much name our price. Freddie in sales is shopping for a new BMW, he's so confident this is going to be his big payoff. This 'death' thing is a stroke of genius. You should go into marketing."

And spend even more time with people like you, I thought. I'd rather eat digitalis cheesecake. I enjoyed having Pudge over the fire, so I rotated the spit a little.

"Well, I think we need to automate the show. People just love spending the night on hold." I was about to fan the flames a little more when smugness crept like a shadow across his doughy face.

"Oh, by the way," he interrupted, with an undisguised note of glee, "there's a policeman waiting in the lounge to see you. I hope you're not into those awful drugs again."

I'd been expecting this. The cops were slow in this town, but even they could follow a beacon like the one my show had become. I flipped Pudge a finger and walked past the studio into the lounge. At the table sat a short, wiry man in a rumpled tan suit. His eyes were beady and intelligent, like those of a field mouse. He was eating a glazed donut.

"You must be Mickey," he said, a jawful of pastry muffling his words. "I'm Detective Dietz from homicide."

He held out his hand for me to shake. My hand came away a little bit sticky.

"I've heard that you might know a little bit about this 'Night Owl' character. According to witnesses, she's called here at the station on at least two occasions, apparently just after committing murder."

"I can't control what people are going to say. There's that little matter of the First Amendment."

"There's also a matter called 'withholding evidence,' and its kissing cousin, 'aiding and abetting.' Surely you're familiar with the judicial system by now."

I was about to protest when he held up a hand. "Society considers those debts paid, Mickey. Or should I say 'Michel'? We just want to stop the killings. All this city needs is a female Charles Bronson running wild. The next thing you know, the papers pick up on it and we got a slew of imitators."

"You already know as much as I do. She says she killed some guys who did her wrong."

"Well, she seems to think you're on her side. You haven't done anything to encourage her, have you?" Dietz wiped the crumbs off his chin and licked his rodent lips.

"Look, she's good for ratings. The audience loves her. She connects with people. Maybe there's a murderous streak in all of us. It's not my place to censor immorality."

"That's why there's a Federal Communications Commission, my friend. I'd be willing to bet that a death forum is not what they consider 'in the public interest.'"

"What can I do?" I shrugged. I got the impression that Dietz would be on me like a fly on stink until he wrapped up this case.

"We want to set up a wire-tap in the studio and wait for her to call again. You'll need to keep her going long enough for us to get a trace. Our technician tells me that takes about two minutes if she's on a local exchange."

I shrugged again. He would have no problem getting a court order if necessary. "I never know when she's going to call."

"We'll wait. We're on salary. And you have good donuts here. We start tonight."

My Honda broke down, so I had to catch a bus back to WKIK that night. As I walked to the entrance, I noticed a sign with my name on it. It was a good space, right next to the GM's. I noted with satisfaction that it was a little closer to the door than Pudge's.

It was a little past midnight, so I was late signing on. Dietz and an engineer who looked like a junkie were already on the job. The engineer was splicing into the phone system. Bits of bare wire littered the floor like copper worms.

I checked the transmitter readings and apologized to the jock who had to stay late to cover for me. He had a little acne around his mouth. Probably an intern. He looked at me with a flash of something like hero worship in his eyes.

"No problem, Mr. Nixon," he said, handing me the playlist. For a second, I thought he was going to ask for my autograph.

I settled behind the console like a pilot about to launch a jumbo jet. Dietz slouched in one corner with a Styrofoam cup of coffee. The engineer held an earphone against his gaunt head and nodded at him. All systems go, prepare for lift-off, I said to myself. I flipped over the mic key and addressed the waiting ears of Topeka.

"Have some fear, Mickey's here, welcome to 'Death Radio,' only on the Kick. Give me a buzz and let me know what's going down in the dark corners of your mind."

I grinned at Dietz as the board lit up. "Go ahead, caller. You're on," I said, cranking up the pot.

A woman with a stuffy nose began talking. "Mickey, I just wanted you to know how much we love 'Death Radio' here at Floyd's Truck Stop. You don't know how many loafers sit around here on their lazy hind ends soppin' up free refills and listenin' to your show."

"Glad to have you aboard, honey. So, have you killed anybody lately?"

I saw Dietz wince as she laughed. "Now, I don't think that girl's as bad as all that. So she shot a few, sounds to me like they had it comin'. And all the guys around here been tippin' real good this week. Been mindin' their manners, and eatin' with their hats off. Ever bad wind blows somebody good, I say."

"Amen to that," I said. I was beginning to wonder, and not for the first time, if I was playing to people's fears just to be a big shot. To be honest with myself, I was enjoying the success. Let people die if it was good for the ratings. I was beginning to think like a television news producer. Give the people what they want and damn the consequences.

I steadily punched up callers, and every one had a story about some man they knew who was finally shaping up or had died trying. A few knew, "first-hand", about somebody who met their Maker over a little marital indiscretion. Dietz was pale, furiously scribbling on a note pad with the stub of a pencil. He hadn't realized just how out of control the show had gotten.

"Folks, I love you," I said at the end of the shift. "Thanks for opening your hearts to me, not to mention a few holes in people's heads. Night Owl, if you're out there, fly right and keep your barrel smoking. Tune in again tomorrow, skip work if you feel like it, and deep-six somebody if you must. This is Mickey Nixon, stick a fork in me, I'm done."

Dietz was as white as a nurse's bra. He would probably be in an all-day powwow with the District Attorney's office, scrambling for offenses to charge me with. Georgie Boy walked in and surveyed the electronic carnage the police engineer had inflicted. I winked at him and poked the Denon machine with my finger. The Cars started playing "Let The Good Times Roll."

Three nights passed that way, with Dietz as my co-pilot and the skeletal technician as navigator. The phone lines stayed busy. Other stations were covering my show as a news event, and a few were trying their own Death Shows. But I was the only one with Night Owl. She called that Tuesday at about 4 AM, just after the hourly station ID.

"Hey, Mickey, honey, it's Night Owl," her voice purred over the speakers.

Dietz jumped up, spilling his coffee and adding another stain to the studio floor. The police tech rolled the tape recorder and watched his meters. I reached a trembling finger to my mic switch.

"Hello, Night Owl, it's good to hear your voice. I was

beginning to think you'd forgotten old Mickey here."

"I'd never do that. Just thinking about you gets me all hot and bothered. I've been listening, and I like what I hear. It seems like murder's the biggest game in town."

"Yes, but nobody does it like you. Have you done it lately?"

"Well, now that you mention it, I was just with a gentleman who knows how to show a lady a good time. He even did the driving. It's funny how if you walk down certain streets at night, guys just pull over and ask if you want a ride. They'll even try to give you money. But, oh my, the things they ask you to do."

"What did this one want?" I was excited and scared at the same time. Dietz flicked his eyes from the tech to his wristwatch, then to my sweaty face.

"You know I don't talk dirty over the phone, Mickey. That would be unladylike. Let's just say we wound up on a dead-end road. I could feel the pounding of his cheap heart beneath his polyester suit. He said I could do it any way I wanted. The way I wanted was to put it right between his meaty chins and scatter his pea-sized brain all over his nice, clean upholstery."

"Way to go, girl," I said. The switchboard was clogged with callers wanting to talk to Night Owl. There was no time to punch someone in. The tech started nodding down the seconds, his bony head wobbling like a frog on a wire, and I felt dread squeeze my throat.

"Mickey, nobody knows how to treat a lady anymore, except you. Thanks for keeping me going when the rest of the world is going crazy. If only every man were like you—"

I suddenly felt sick.

"Hang up, there's a police trace!" I screamed into my

mic, covering it with saliva. I heard a click on the monitors. It was the sound of my world coming to an end, in a stream of dead air instead of the guitar feedback I'd always imagined.

Dietz rushed at me, anger twisting his face into a mask. The tech threw his scrawny arms up in surrender. I leaned back in my swivel chair and stared at the zeroed-out volume meters. "Good-bye, Night Owl," I said, to no one in particular.

Everything moved in slow motion after that. Dietz read me my rights and was about to snap on the cuffs, but in my condition, I was about as dangerous as a goldfish. Once he regained his composure, he was kind enough to let me run the board until another jock showed up. They couldn't reach Pudge, but the GM sent in the pimply intern. I signed off with The Who's "Song is Over."

I've got a battery of lawyers from the American Civil Liberties Union, and they tell me my case will be tied up for years, years I probably don't have. Night Owl left a message on my answering machine at home.

"Mickey, you said you'd never do me wrong, but you're just like all the rest." Sadness had replaced the fire in her voice, and her words twisted in my chest like a corkscrew. "All the joy's gone, but at least I still have my work. I'll see you around. And now I think I'm supposed to say, 'Don't call me, I'll call you.'"

I kept my deejay job. There was no one to fire me. It seems Pudge was found dead in his car. Ballistics tests match those of the other Night Owl murders. The GM decided I have just enough notoriety left to draw a few listeners. They've removed the interface from the studio, and all we have is a request line.

So now I sit and wait. I heard there's been a string of

shootings over in Council Bluffs, with a familiar M.O., and it's not a long drive to get here. The request line blinks, as lonely as the last morning star. Wayne is on the other end.

"Looks like it's just you and me," I say.

"Rock on, dude."

I do.

In The Heart of November

Margaret sat on the tombstone, swinging her legs.

Ellen could read Margaret's name carved in the gray granite, though the letters were blurred. "How long have we been friends?" Margaret asked, her voice like a lost wind.

"You mean...before or after?" Ellen pulled her sweater more tightly across her chest. The graveyard was in the heart of November, all shadow and chill and flapping brown leaves.

"Both, silly."

"Seven years."

"And have I ever broken a promise or blabbed a secret?"

Ellen looked away. Even though Margaret was almost invisible, her eyes glowed bright and strange. Ellen had stopped by the graveyard every day after school since her best friend had been buried, and they often spent hours out here in the summer, talking about boys and Ellen's mom and Mrs. Deerfield's geometry tests. Margaret knew more of Ellen's secrets than anybody.

"I don't know," Ellen said. "You never blab on this side,

but you could be telling my secrets to every dead person in the world, for all I know."

Margaret's wispy features darkened. "Dead people don't care about your problems. They've got their own."

"Their problems can't be as bad as mine."

Margaret drifted down from the tombstone and put a cold hand on Ellen's shoulder. "I wish you would never have to find out."

"If I were dead, then it wouldn't matter if boys treated me like I was dirt."

"Don't be so sure."

"Do boys like you...over *there*?" Ellen tried to picture Doug as a ghost, but couldn't. He was too tall and healthy and strong. He was meant to be running up and down a soccer field, as swift as sunshine, his dark curly hair flying about his face.

"Dead boys just aren't very interesting," Margaret said. "They don't want to do anything but sleep."

Margaret put her hands together, and the pale fingers merged. "It's hard to hold hands when you don't have much to hang on to. And kissing—" Margaret puckered her lips and made an exaggerated smacking sound. "Nobody likes cold lips."

"Gross," said Ellen.

Margaret's giggle spilled out over the grass and echoed off the stone wall that surrounded the cemetery. The sun was sinking into the gnarled tops of trees. Cars passed by the highway beyond the wall, the wheels making whispers on the asphalt.

"I'd better get home," Ellen said. "Mom will be mad."

"I wish you could stay here all the time."

"But you don't want me to be dead."

"I just get lonely sometimes. Lonely for living people. I

miss being alive."

Ellen looked into Margaret's unearthly eyes. "You miss Doug."

"Wouldn't you?"

Ellen didn't say anything. How could she tell her best friend that they were in love with the same guy? She'd hoped Margaret would get over him. Margaret and Doug didn't have anything in common anymore, especially now.

But they had been close once. Back in the seventh grade, they'd been as steady as anybody. And all Ellen could do was watch with envy as they held onto each other at school dances or talked quietly during lunch or passed notes in class. After Margaret was hit by a car and killed, Ellen thought Doug was going to die as well, only from a broken heart instead of a broken body.

"I've got to go," Ellen said. Her mom would yell at her for being late again. If only Mom knew that the more she yelled, the more Ellen wanted to be late. Ellen waved and started through the rows of tombstones.

Margaret followed. "I might come out tomorrow," she said.

Ellen turned, chilled by more than the long shade of a dead oak. "I thought they didn't like it when you come out."

"Who cares what they think?" Margaret shook her see-through hair. "I get tired of them telling me what to do and where to go. They don't want anybody to have any fun."

Ellen didn't know who "they" were, but Margaret's eyes always narrowed with anger when she spoke of them. "You aren't supposed to leave," Ellen said.

"Gosh, you're starting to sound like your mom." Margaret's hollow voice rose in pitch as she mimicked Ellen's mom. "'You were *supposed* to be home an hour ago. You were *supposed* to make an A on that math test.'"

Ellen laughed, even though Margaret's shrill imitation was too perfect, and it reminded Ellen of what was awaiting at home. "What will they do to you if you leave?"

Margaret shrugged. "You don't want to know."

Margaret had left the cemetery once, had floated outside Ellen's window in the mobile home park. This had been about two weeks after her burial. Margaret had seemed so much more lost, lonely, and *creepy* outside of the graveyard. Whatever invisible chains kept her bound to the dirt under her tombstone must have been painful to break, because when Ellen visited the next day, Margaret had faded to nearly nothing. A month passed before Margaret returned to her usual thin form.

Ellen moved to her best friend and gave her a hug. At least, she tried. Her arms passed through Margaret, raising goosebumps. "Don't do anything to make them mad. They might take you forever next time."

"I want to see Doug," Margaret said.

"Doug's not worth it."

"How do you know? What do *you* know about losing somebody you love?"

Ellen's eyes grew hot with held tears. Margaret was beautiful. She could have had any boy she wanted. Ellen was afraid that Margaret still could, even dead. "I've really got to go."

"I'm sorry. I wasn't trying to be mean."

Ellen sniffled. "It's not your fault. I'm just feeling sorry for myself."

"See you tomorrow?"

Ellen nodded and hurried from the graveyard, making sure no one was looking before she climbed over the cemetery wall. She slipped into the woods and onto the well-worn path that led home.

"What's wrong?" Mom asked. "You've hardly eaten a bite. You're not going to starve yourself so you can look like the girls in *Seventeen*, are you? I told you to quit wasting money on those stupid magazines."

"No, Mom, I'm not on a diet." Ellen was tired of eating macaroni and cheese and greasy hamburger. Mom's cooking even made the school cafeteria lunches look good.

"You look pale." Mom leaned over the small table and pressed her hand to Ellen's forehead. Her hand was nearly as cold as Margaret's. "You're not taking sick, are you?"

"I feel fine." Except her belly was like a nest of snakes. She was worried that Margaret would come out tomorrow.

"Well, you don't *look* fine."

"I think I just want to go lie down a while."

"Got your homework done?"

Ellen nodded. She always did her homework while the teachers were explaining it to the rest of the class. Margaret had gotten beauty, but Ellen was lucky with books. Too bad Doug was smart, too, and never asked Ellen to help him with homework.

"Well, good. That's one less thing I've got to worry about." Mom's face was pinched and tired, her cheeks flushed. She might have been drinking. Ellen couldn't smell anything over the cloying aroma of cheese powder.

Ellen pushed her plate away, knowing she'd see the leftovers again tomorrow. And tomorrow might bring other horrors. She went down the narrow paneled hall to her bedroom. The bed took up most of the floor, and she crawled onto it and lay on her back, looking at the pictures of musicians and unicorns on her walls. The unicorns would have to go. She was getting too old for unicorns.

She reached over, slid her desk drawer open, and took out the photograph. Its edges were worn from handling, but the face was just as wonderful as always. Doug smiled out from between the white borders, straight teeth and dark eyes and curly hair. Something swished against the window, and Ellen's breath froze in her lungs. What if Margaret was at her window, looking in? What if Margaret had seen her gazing longingly at Doug's picture?

She got on her knees and looked out the window. The lights blazed in the windows of the mobile homes, which were arranged as awkwardly as tombstones. Different sizes, moved in at different times, all slowly fading under the wear of time. This was her graveyard, and she was as trapped here as Margaret was in the graveyard of grass and granite and artificial flowers.

Nobody stirred outside, neither the dead nor the living. Leaves scurried across the bare yards like frantic mice. A pole at the end of the park glowed with a sick blue light, but it was too cold and weak to attract bugs. Ellen drew her curtains tight and rested back on her pillow.

Doug. He'd said hello to her in the hall the other day. She summoned the memory in all its glory, the flash of his eyes, the warm tone of his voice, his head above the crowd of students changing class. She'd been too nervous to say anything in response, all she could do was give a lame wave and what she hoped was a smile.

Probably looked like a grimace. She brought a small hand mirror from her drawer and practiced her smile. Dimples that were dumpy instead of cute. Her cheeks were fat. She had a pimple on her chin. God, she was *hideous*. No wonder Doug didn't want her.

She and Doug had been close briefly, right after Margaret's death. They had sat together at lunch, Doug wearing sunglasses so that no one could tell that Mr. Cool had been crying. They'd even hugged at the funeral, and now Ellen embraced that fleeting memory of his muscles.

If only Margaret could die every day, then maybe Doug and I—

As soon as she had the thought, she was sickened. She'd rather have Margaret back alive than to have any guy in the world. Anyway, if Margaret were alive, Doug would still be going out with her. Margaret had been beautiful. Still was. And Ellen was a frumpy, dumpy piece of nobody. She cried herself to a restless sleep.

"You didn't come out," Ellen said the next afternoon.

Margaret lowered her voice, looking around at the other graves. "I was scared."

"I don't blame you." Ellen felt a small spark of joy, a lightness in her chest. If Margaret didn't go out, everything would be okay.

"I want to see him."

"You'd better be careful, Margaret."

"I don't have to talk to him or anything. I just want to *see* him. To remember what he's like."

"What about Doug? What if you freak him out?"

"I didn't freak *you* out."

"Well, you did a little, at first. I mean, it's not like I believed in ghosts or anything, or did one of those corny seances to try and bring you back."

"I wonder if Doug misses me as much as I miss him."

Ellen didn't know whether to lie or not. She had never kept secrets from Margaret before. She looked at the ground, at the seam of stubborn dirt where the grass hadn't taken root.

"Are you ashamed of having me for a friend?" Margaret asked.

"Of course not." Ellen knelt in the moist grass by the tombstone. "You'll always be my best friend. Forever."

"Better than Doug?"

Does she know? Ellen's throat was tight. *What would a ghost do to you if you tried to steal her boyfriend?*

"Doug still thinks about you a lot," Ellen managed to say, which wasn't a lie. "I talked to him a few weeks ago. He said that you guys listened to Crash Test Dummies together. He said that 'Swimming In Your Ocean' was your favorite song."

"Crash Test Dummies. Now *that's* what I call irony, seeing the way I got killed."

Ellen tried to change the subject away from Doug and death. "Do they have music...over there?"

Margaret looked beyond the graveyard, beyond trees and stone and all things solid, as if she hadn't heard Ellen. "It doesn't hurt to get killed. It hurts more, afterward. Being dead, I mean. And knowing it. That's the worst thing."

"I wish I could trade places with you." So Doug would be in love with *her*. Even if she couldn't do anything about it, couldn't hold his hand or kiss him. She'd be happy enough just to know he carried her in his heart. Just to be able to make him happy or sad when he thought of her.

"Don't say that." Margaret drifted down from the stone. Part of her misty flesh seeped across Ellen's face. Ellen shivered.

"It hurts to be dead, Ellen. It hurts to remember everything you lost."

"You haven't lost me," Ellen said, wondering if Margaret was splashing the chill of death on her face just to warn her. But Ellen would never commit suicide. She was too scared. And if she died, she'd never have Doug. But would Doug have *her*?

"I don't ever want to lose you." Margaret's smile was a white sliver of movement among the smoky threads of her face. The front gate of the cemetery creaked open.

"Somebody's coming," Ellen said, but Margaret had already disappeared, back to her cold and dreamless sleep. Ellen pretended to mumble a prayer in case the visitors happened to see her. Then she went out the front gate and headed toward the soccer field.

Ellen's mom would be mad, but Ellen didn't care. Nothing else mattered anymore. Let everybody else hate her. She had to find out once, for all, and forever.

"This is really weird, Ellen," Doug said.

What did Doug know about weirdness? His world was soccer games, shooting for college scholarships, getting tons of pictures in the yearbook. He'd been in the graveyard before, but not since Margaret's funeral, and certainly never when the sky was purple with sundown. A pale slice of moon hung in bare branches like an ornament.

"How come you've never been back?" Ellen asked.

"Because I—" Doug paused, gasped. "I don't know. It makes me think about her, and I don't like to think about her. It makes my chest hurt."

They stood before Margaret's grave, Doug shivering in his soccer shorts and T-shirt. She'd dragged him here right after practice, had called him to the sidelines and told him she had something really important to show him. So important it couldn't wait for him to get dressed.

She'd taken his hand, and he hadn't pulled away. She led him across the street and over the hill, feeling the eyes of Doug's friends on her back. They probably thought good old Doug was going to score, put another one in the net. Ellen trembled as they walked, brushing aside his questions until they came to the graveyard.

"Margaret is my best friend," Ellen said. Doug looked at her as if she were crazy, but she didn't feel crazy at all. In fact, for the first time in years, she felt that her life was under her own control.

"Yeah, Margaret was great," Doug said, looking around at the tombstones gray in the weak light. "She was really special."

"I have to know, Doug. Did you really love her?"

Doug let go of her hand. "You're scaring me."

"The truth is nothing to be afraid of." Ellen squinted at Margaret's grave, but could see none of the strange milkiness of her ghost. She hoped they hadn't called Margaret away, that they hadn't confined her to some dismal, dark hibernation. *"Did you love her?"*

Doug looked around. He seemed uncomfortable without an audience. Ellen wondered if this was how he acted when he was alone with Margaret. "Uh, yeah. Sure. Of course I did."

"How many girls have you gone out with since then?"

"What's that got to do with anything?"

"It's got everything to do with everything."

"Are you feeling okay?"

"I'm fine." Ellen grinned, not caring if her dimples were dumpy. "Never been better. How many girls?"

"Heck, I don't know. Five, six."

"Maybe ten?"

"Maybe."

"And you loved Margaret the best?"

"You're weird. I've got to go."

"Just answer me, and you can leave."

He scratched his head. His eyes reflected the moonlight. "Well, I loved her. But you got to move on. You got to keep living. I know you were her best friend, but I didn't know you were so hung up on her."

"Even dead people have feelings." She almost wished Margaret would rise like fog, to tell Doug how much she missed him. Ellen wondered how Mr. Cool would handle *that*.

"I'm getting out of here."

Doug headed for the gate, hunched, his arms huddled across his chest. November was always cold, especially in the graveyard. But Ellen knew some things were colder than November. Like a guy's heart.

"She loved you, you know," Ellen called.

Doug stopped near the gate, his shadow mingling with the wrought-iron bars. "I thought you were taking me out here so we could be alone. I was going to kiss you. I was going to be gentle. I was even going to walk you home after."

"I bet you say that to all the girls," Margaret said, her voice everywhere and nowhere.

Doug glanced at the sky, shook his head as if to clear away cobwebs or memories or imagined voices, then hurried through the gate.

"He's not so hot after all," Margaret said from her tombstone perch. "Not like I remember him."

Ellen turned, wondering how long Margaret had been sitting there. "Some people grow on you, and some don't."

"You could have fallen in love with him," Margaret said. "I wouldn't have minded too much."

"I know. But every time I kissed him, I would have

thought of you. And he wouldn't have."

"Yeah." The moon shone into Margaret, making her hair radiant. She was beautiful, both inside and outside. "Well, when you're dead, warm lips are gross anyway."

They shared a laugh, and even though the wind howled around them, Ellen was warm. She might not know what losing love was like, but she knew what *having* it was like.

"You'd better get home," Margaret said. "Your mom's going to kill you."

"Naw. She's not going to kill me. I'm going to live a long time."

The cemetery was silent except for the brittle rattling of bone-dry leaves. After a moment, Margaret said, "Live for both of us, okay?"

Ellen reached out, held the wispy hand of her best friend. "I promise," she whispered.

Ellen left Margaret to her dark sleep and headed for the gate, street, and home. Tomorrow Doug would be telling half the school that she was nuts, but she didn't care. Doug could go stuff himself, as far as she was concerned. She could hardly wait to get home and tear his picture into shreds.

There was one more thing. She paused at the gate. "See you tomorrow, Margaret," she called across the empty graveyard.

A peaceful hush was her only answer.

The Three-Dollar Corpse

The morning sky was red-orange, the colors of hell and Georgia August. Ragsdale squinted into the brightness and marveled at how rapidly the scant dew had evaporated. Another fifty men would die today, but that was today. At the moment, the only dead that Ragsdale cared about were yesterday's.

The corpses were in a line, laid out like sacks of grain. Some had been stripped of their rotted clothing, leaving pale skin stretched taut over bones, flesh exposed to the unblinking eye of dawn. Others, treated more mercifully, had scraps of blankets covering their rigid faces. Those lucky souls were tended by friends. The rest were accompanied by traders like Ragsdale.

Ragsdale could see Tibbets' corpse, down at the end of the row where the freshest ones were. He mourned the waste of a good body. As a tentmate of Tibbets, Ragsdale had a right to be the one who bore the corpse to the dead-house. But a corpse at the end of the line was nearly worthless, and brought only fifty cents for the privilege of carrying it out. So he'd sold the privilege and bought the three-dollar corpse at the front of the line.

Those near the front of the line had first chances with the smugglers waiting in the woods beyond the stockade walls. A good day of trading kept one's belly full and made a handful of dollars besides. The war would end someday, and Ragsdale planned on having a small fortune tucked away inside his boots the day he walked out of the camp for good.

Some of the soldiers freely distributed their smuggled goods to keep others alive. Ragsdale didn't believe in camaraderie. Only each man to himself, each man to live or die as his wits allowed, each man abandoned and alone, even though 40,000 of them were cramped into a place barely 25 acres across. And each death was welcomed, if not by the poor sufferer himself, then certainly by the huckster tradesmen like Ragsdale.

He held his kerchief over his face to block out the wave of corrupted air, but the kerchief smelled as bad as the bodies. He had once used the kerchief to filter the water from the sluggish stream that served as both drinking supply and sewage for the prisoners in the Andersonville camp. Even after several strainings, the water still looked like tea in the bottom of his dented tin cup. But all he could do was grimace and swallow, the fetid particles imparting a sweetly foul aftertaste. Ever since he'd become a huckster, though, he had all the fresh water he could drink.

"You see Tibbets go over?" It was McCloskey, a young tough who had the corpse next to Ragsdale's. McCloskey had been working his way up the line over the last few weeks, a sign of affluence. Ragsdale didn't like the competition. McCloskey was starting to get some of the better trade goods, things like cigars and real bread and even an occasional pint of whiskey. *Damned Irish*, Ragsdale thought. But he kept his face as stolid as those of the dead.

"Yeah," Ragsdale said, quietly, so that the guards assembled by the gate didn't snarl at him. "I wish I coulda got that fresh one instead of this here sorry sack of maggots." Ragsdale nudged the corpse with his boots.

"You got the first one," McCloskey said. "Every first one is beautiful."

"Maybe. Damn shame about Tibbets, though." What Ragsdale meant was that if Tibbets had any consideration, he'd have died early in the day so that Ragsdale could have made more profit from his corpse.

Tibbets was from the 82nd Regiment New York Volunteers, the same as Ragsdale. Tibbets was the religious sort, always chattering in his sleep about the divine hand of God that would deliver him from suffering. He never bothered to make any money, and never asked Ragsdale for extra portions, though the smell of smuggled food must have been overpowering in that small tent. Maybe he knew Ragsdale would have denied him.

So Tibbets wasted away on camp rations and prayer, until the previous evening. He had eaten his palmful of raw corn meal, not even bothering to pick the larger pieces of dry cob from the ration. Soon the food was gone, leaving only a few white specks in Tibbet's beard, his lips being too dry for the meal to stick. But the fool had not stopped there. He continued gnawing at the toughened skin of his fingers, perhaps imagining them to be fine Illinois sausages.

Ragsdale had slapped Tibbets' hand away, but the man's jaws continued to gnash together. Those teeth rattled like sabers, a percussive counterpoint to the low somber dirge made by the groans of ten thousand sick, wounded, and dying. Tibbets' eyes went bright and wide, looking past the high stockade walls and the coarse Southern clouds to that high place where He was trampling out the vintages. Before Ragsdale could stop Tibbets, if he had even thought to stop him, the man had vaulted to his feet and dashed through the rows of ragged tents.

The stricken man was all bony limbs and rags, jerking like a windy scarecrow on a wire. The nearby prisoners paused in the eating of their rations to watch him run. Shouts arose, half of the voices pleading for him to stop, the other half urging him onward. They all, Ragsdale included, watched as Tibbets neared the slim gray railing that marked the dead line.

The dead line was a single wooden rail laid about twenty feet inside the walls and circumscribing the perimeter of the camp. Any prisoner who crossed the rail was assumed to be attempting escape, and was instantly shot. It was the only activity that kept the Rebel guards alert, for they had been denied the glory of battle by their ignominious posts. A Union prisoner might be their only quarry of the war, so they competed among themselves to be the one who fired a successful shot.

Three rifles rang out as Tibbets vaulted the fence. Tibbets stumbled, fell to one knee, then rose and continued staggering toward the stockade wall. Maybe his fevered brain thought that reaching the wooden wall itself was some kind of victory, as if a door might open and usher him to Elysian fields. In any case, Tibbets fell dead when a fourth shot pierced his skull.

But he'd died in the evening, and a whole day's dispatch of dead were already waiting to be carried outside before him. So Tibbets lay stiff and nearly worthless near the end of the line, attended by some amateur hucksters who were no competition to the likes of Ragsdale and McCloskey.

"What got yours?" McCloskey said, biting off a small

plug of chewing tobacco. Ragsdale watched him with disguised envy, then looked down at the corpse at his feet. The flesh around the sunken eyes was as black as the inside of coalstove pipe.

"Dysentery, diarrhea, the Tennessee trots, take your pick."

"At least the lice is off him, eh?" McCloskey cackled juicily around his chaw.

"Every dark cloud," Ragsdale said, tired of talking. But McCloskey was right. If you happened to be near a man at the moment the heat started fading from his dead body, all the fleas and lice and invisible parasites hopped and jumped onto the closest host. Ragsdale scratched his beard, remembering the things crawling there.

He looked off toward the center of the camp, at the stretch of swamp that served as the camp's sewer. A few men were in the thick of the morass, relieving themselves. A new prisoner stood at the edge, his face curdled in horror at what the others had accepted as routine. The surface of the swamp churned with the breeding of maggots. Ragsdale looked away as the new prisoner squatted at the edge of the soiled water.

The front gate opened, and a half-dozen Rebels slouched in, their guns lazily angled toward the ground. They were near-corpses themselves, gray-faced and war-weary and noses wrinkled against the constant fecal rot of the camp. A captain accompanied them, head high, wearing leather leggings and his brass polished and gleaming in the dawn. Ragsdale cursed under his breath.

This was the man whose pockets were filled by the mass misery. But Ragsdale knew he was no more honorable himself. He only begrudged the captain skimming off the profits, and avoided all reflections on morality. Now, with the guard coming, he thought of nothing but the tradesmen waiting outside, the smugglers and dealers waiting along the route to the deadhouse and the grave ditch.

And he had first opportunity. Sure, it cost him a good thirty percent of his take, but he was making a killing inside the stockade. He was fat, which was a prisoner's true sign of wealth. He had clean water and cotton blankets and molasses and pipe tobacco. He had a pillow. And no one would touch him, because to cross Ragsdale meant getting no smuggled goods, subsisting on the meager camp rations, and likely a slow death.

The Rebel captain gave the command for the detail to move out. Ragsdale lifted his corpse with ease. The fellow was hardly more than a skeleton. That was another advantage of a disease victim. With fresh ones like Tibbets, two men had to carry the corpse on a makeshift stretcher, which split the profits.

Ragsdale dragged the corpse past the open dead line toward the gates. The guards watched, hollow-eyed, not even joyful about the goods that the hucksters would slip them upon the return trip. They were as much prisoners of war as the Union troops. All were bound to this boiling swamp of disease and death, and sometimes Ragsdale could imagine the war never ending, their ghost-like daily struggles extending into an afterlife of misery.

He never imagined anything for long, though. In the camp, dreams were dangerous. If you dreamed, you were apt to lose your reason. That was one of the few differences between the living and the dead: only the dead could afford to dream.

So he shook his head and damned himself for dreaming. All one had to do was look back toward the camp, at the pathetic shebangs made of old coats and tent scraps and dry tree limbs, with not even enough of a breeze to flutter a stray thread. And in front of the makeshift tents, or dying inside them, were men. Men who had letters from home folded carefully in their pockets, men with children waiting, men with hearts swollen by religious faith and patriotism and all false hopes.

Ragsdale smiled to himself. He wouldn't cling to bravery. He would survive. He pulled the corpse through the gates.

The captain nodded as Ragsdale passed.

"Morning, Johnny," Ragsdale said, using the only term of address that the prisoners were allowed.

"Going to be a dandy one, Yank. Don't ya'll forget me on the way back in."

"No, suh," Ragsdale said, imitating a Southern accent. He kept his grin plastered on, and wondered if that was how the Negroes felt, smiling and smiling as the lash came down across their backs. He didn't know, because he'd never met one.

The haul to the dead-house was about a hundred yards. The corpse-bearers passed the cookhouse on the way, and a charred smell drowned out the rot of corpses. A gaunt civilian came from the cookhouse and dumped a thick greasy liquid into the stream. Ragsdale watched the gray slick make its way down the creek towards the stockade.

When Ragsdale reached the dead-house, which was an open covered area, he laid the corpse down and went into the shade of the high Georgia pines. The other hucksters laid out their corpses as well. In the dead-house, Confederate officials tried to determine the names and units of the dead and keep careful records. But as the death tolls mounted over the summer, the effort had become hurried and careless.

But, brief though the respite was, there was time enough for Ragsdale to do business.

"Hi, Johnny," Ragsdale said to the Rebel guard who was slouched against a tree. The guard might have been a civilian from the manner of dress, but Ragsdale took no chances.

"Howdy." The guard scarcely looked up. "Don't you go and try to run, or I got to put a bullet in your back."

"Wouldn't dream of it, Johnny." And he wouldn't. He was making too much money. "What's good today?"

"Hear tell there's some sweet potatoes. Smoked pork, too. Eggs."

Eggs. A good egg could fetch fifty cents, a rotten egg a dime. Ragsdale smiled and reached inside his shirt, which was overlarge and worn loose so that he could smuggle as many items as possible back into camp. He pulled a small sack of dried beans from a hidden pocket and passed it to the Rebel.

"Much obliged," the guard said, without looking up. Ragsdale hurried into the trees. McCloskey and the other hucksters would be along soon, and Ragsdale wanted his choice of merchandise. He was scarcely twenty feet into the forest when a man stepped out of the brush.

Their eyes met. The man held out his hands, revealing four small brown eggs.

"How much?"

"A quarter," the man said. Deal done. Ragsdale then purchased some stale tobacco, pork that had not yet gone rancid in the heat, a dozen wrinkled potatoes. All for a dollar, which he would turn into ten dollars on the inside, and have a full belly besides. He put the goods inside his clothes, except for the eggs, which he wanted to protect until all the bodies were counted and it was time to bury the three-dollar corpse.

He started back toward the dead-house, pleased with

his purchases. Another man stepped from the trees.

"Sorry, Johnny, all done up," Ragsdale said.

"That's a shame," the man said. "Because I got quality goods."

Ragsdale glanced at the face. That dark hair, those bright eyes—

Ragsdale nearly dropped his eggs. Tibbets stood before him, smiling.

"Yeah, it's me." Tibbets' mouth yawned open in speaking, and Ragsdale saw where the fatal bullet had shattered the man's jaw. Ragsdale felt the blood drain from his face. His mind screamed at him to run, but his legs were rooted to the Georgia clay.

"Nuh—," Ragsdale grunted, unable to formulate any words which would explain the impossibility before him. It was Tibbets, all right, fevered and pale and exactly the same as he had been yesterday, with the exception of the bloody holes in his worn tunic.

"It's better out here," Tibbets said, again flapping the damaged lips. "Look."

The dead man held out his thin hands, palms full of pink soap and razors and fine Illinois sausage and eggs the size of apples. Despite his shock, Ragsdale couldn't help coveting the merchandise.

It's a dream, Ragsdale said to himself. *My belly's full and I'm dozing in the shade of my tent.*

But the fine fragrance of the soap beckoned him, too real for dreams, more vivid than any sensation he had ever known. He reached for it. "How much?" he managed to gasp.

Tibbets pulled the goods back into the folds of his tunic. "Not for sale."

Not for sale? Why, everything was for sale, ever since

those 3,000 Plymouth prisoners had been brought in. Just before their capture, they'd been furloughed from the Union army, and under the terms of their conditional surrender, they were allowed to keep the veteran's bounty that filled their pockets, hundreds of dollars per man. Since then, the huckster business was booming.

And Tibbets wasn't going to deny him what was rightfully his. He'd paid his three dollars for that first corpse, he'd bribed his captors, he'd earned first chances on the merchandise fair and square. What was it to Ragsdale if some men starved because they couldn't afford his mark-up?

"That soap," Ragsdale said. Imagine the luxury of soap in a camp where the prisoners waded into an open swamp to relieve themselves? Where the odor of fevered sweat and gangrenous flesh and death, death, death, hung in the air like a solid thing? Who wouldn't want to scrub such misery from their skin? Why, soap would fetch five dollars a bar.

"You can have all this," Tibbets said. "And more."

"More?"

"Pumpkin and corn, raspberries, honey, sugar, coffee. All free."

As if by magic, what had to be magic, the scent of those products wended into Ragsdale's nostrils. How long since he had tasted real coffee? Chickamauga, nearly a year ago?

There was a crashing in the brush nearby, and he knew that the guard had come to herd the hucksters back to the dead-house. Only moments to act. He knew he must be mad, and that Tibbets couldn't exist. Still, those smells haunted him as no mere ghost could.

"Yank?" called the guard from beyond the trees.

Ragsdale leaned toward Tibbets and whispered. "How?"

"Cross the dead line," Tibbets said, his ragged lips stretching into a smile. "It's all here waiting. We've got a camp set up behind the forest."

And as the Rebel guard blundered cursing through the bushes, Tibbets vanished back into the pines. Ragsdale gave the guard an egg to soothe the man's anger, then allowed himself to be led back to the dead-house. All the while, Ragsdale thought of those smells, tried to recall them and keep them full in his mind.

As he dragged the three-dollar corpse from the dead-house to the grave ditch, he looked at the others with their corpses and searched madly for Tibbets. Ragsdale and the others stooped and strained with their shovels, widening the ditch to add their fifty to the thousands already returned to the soil. McCloskey was digging beside him, stripped to the waist, the sheen of sweat bright on his muscles.

"McCloskey, have you seen Tibbets?"

"Tibbets? Who cares about Tibbets? I've got a pound of tobacco to sell when we get back inside."

Then the deed was done, the bodies covered but the ditch still open and awaiting tomorrow's supply. As they went back to the stockade and again entered that dreary mass of groaning men, Ragsdale could take no joy in his smuggled goods. He gave the captain an egg, then went among the disease and squalor and filth and sat in his tent, thinking of orange pumpkins and strong coffee and, most of all, that sweet, sweet soap.

The afternoon came and two dozen died in the heat. Evening food rations were parceled out. Still Ragsdale sat, heedless of the eggs and potatoes in the folds of his shirt. The prisoners who eagerly came to him with cash were sent away grumbling about how smugglers held out on goods to drive up the price. But Ragsdale cared nothing for their money. Because out there, in the high bristling trees beyond the stockade walls, was soap and coffee and bacon and perhaps a pint of fine bourbon.

All he had to do was cross the dead line.

He stood on trembling legs. His eyes were bright and looking toward where vintages might need stamping.

As he broke into a run, he heard shouts erupt from the tents, and from the little circles of men gathered around their cooking fires. But he didn't stop, he didn't even hear them, and then he saw what Tibbets must have seen.

A large shining field, rolling out in gold and green and red, all harvest colors. And to the sides, under shady trees, were stalls and wagons loaded with every luxury known to civilized man. Crisp tents and bright campfires stretched into the distance, and the smell of frying bacon mingled with the woodsmoke.

Ragsdale vaulted the rail and shouts rang from above. Still he ran, the blood roaring in his ears. A wetness poured down his head, surrounded him, and he lost his balance as darkness fell.

Dawn found him outside the walls. He searched for Tibbets, but saw nothing but scrub forest. Sounds from the prison gate drew him back to the edge of the woods. The grave detail was heading out. Ragsdale thought that McCloskey would take his place at the front of the line, but all the prisoners were strangers.

Ragsdale saw his own corpse down near the end of the line. A fifty-cent corpse. He looked hopefully at the two hard-eyed Union prisoners that carried the flesh that Ragsdale had so recently worn. Ragsdale was annoyed that someone had made fifty cents off his corpse. That money was rightfully his.

Maybe he could hail the soldiers, send them away with

a quick profit and no work. Ragsdale searched his boots for money and found none. Someone had robbed him as he lay dead. And he had nothing to trade. He watched from the woods as his body was counted, then thrown in the ditch and buried.

As the dirt was thrown over his face, night fell, then the sun rose and found him watching the next grave detail. Again his corpse was dragged before his eyes. A different pair of soldiers carried him that morning. He again felt the anger at someone profiting from his death.

A week of such dawns, a month of funeral processions, and Ragsdale became accustomed to the stench of corpses. In fact, he welcomed it. Because the stench helped drown out the maddening aromas that drifted through the trees, the exotic smells of soap and coffee and bacon, goods that were being enjoyed by others in peaceful distant bivouacs. If only Ragsdale had some money, he might go there and trade in the land where everything was free.

Sometimes, just as the dirt was thrown on the face of his corpse and night again fell, he heard laughter and singing from the far camps. It was the sound of men with full bellies.

A year passed, and Ragsdale still had no money, not even the fifty cents that his bullet-riddled corpse brought each day. He sat and watched the grave details, his stomach rumbling with an emptiness greater than hunger.

Ten, twenty, a hundred years of soft parades.

In the trees, forever in sight of the stockade walls, Ragsdale waited for the war to end.

Thirst

Sally hadn't rained in days.

She hid under the porch when Mom opened the screen door. The wood of the porch bent and groaned above her head. Mom's shadow fell across the sunlit cracks between the boards, and Sally knew it was time. She hated being one of the stupid old rain people.

She wanted to be like Melanie, with a blue dress and fine yellow hair and no freckles and skin that didn't turn pink on the first spring day. But Mom said Sally was a rain girl, and that was that. Rain girls weren't supposed to be pretty, even with rainbows in their hair.

And raining was so much trouble. How could you have fun when you had to fight the sun and mash the clouds together and wring the drops out of the sky? She had to worry about the trees, the flowers and shrubs and vines and thorns and all of them screaming and whining for water. And the people, too. Mom had told her a million times that she had to care about people she didn't even know. Stupid people with their stupid thirsts.

It was so grown-up, all this worry. She wanted to spend her summer catching the frogs that hid in the grass beside the ditch, racing boys down the street on her bicycle, running through butterfly fields with her arms spread wide as the colors dodged and blurred at the edge of her vision. She longed to sit under the stars at the foot of an old oak and just breathe the big air and not think about whether the soil was moist enough. She wanted summer nights, holding hands with Jason if she could gather the nerve.

"Come help me, Sally Ann," Mom called. "Got chores to do."

Mom was on the porch steps now, and Sally could see the veins in her ankles. Mom was dehydrating. Her eyes were faded and rinsed, her face creased with arid distress, her hands cracked like an ancient washwoman's. Mom had started driving the rain at an early age, younger even than Sally. And now she was worn, shriveled, like a sponge that had soaked up too many spills.

The shady space under the porch was a tiny separate world. Outside it, the maddening sun baked the earth and asphalt ran like a river between the neighborhood houses. Sally wished she could lie there forever on her belly in the cool dirt. But it was early afternoon in July, and that meant only one thing.

Time for thunderstorms.

"Sally?" Mom called again.

"Coming, Mom." She skinnied out from under the porch, catching a cobweb with one of her pigtails. Her mother smiled down, her lips a pinch of gray.

She's so tired, Sally thought. *Why doesn't she just QUIT?*

"That's my good girl," Mom said.

"It must be time, huh?" Sally sniffed the air for rain,

but it was too early. Mom's eyes were dry.

Mom turned and walked into the house without answering. Sally followed, letting a couple of flies into the house before slamming the screen door closed. She'd heard that flies bit more before a storm, but she didn't believe the saying was true.

Dad was sprawled on the couch, fanning himself with a newspaper. The paper was opened to the sports section. For a spiteful moment, she felt like raining out a few baseball games.

Dad was a demolition man. He ran a wrecking ball and worked as a dynamiter when he had the chance. But there weren't a lot of buildings to tear down in this dying town. Nobody wanted to build here. Too hot. The concrete clung to steel bones and waited, waited, waited, while the windows and doors held their breath.

Mom sat at the table and folded her hands. Sally wished Mom wouldn't wear those ugly scarves on her head. They made her look like a gypsy. People talked enough the way it was, without giving them more whisper ammunition.

Dad rolled to his feet and flapped the papers, then threw them to the floor. He growled and kicked the edge of the couch. Mom closed her eyes and turned down the corners of her mouth and her eyelashes flickered like electric moths. Outside, the sky grew darker.

Across town or country, one of the wind people was at work, sending chapped leaves and candy wrappers skittering across parking lots and sidewalks. Sally sat at the table across from her mother as the breeze rattled the screen door.

Dad pounded the walls with the bottom of his fists.

The sky grew charcoal gray.

Mom whimpered.

A raindrop fell, ticking off the shingles like a small stone.

"Come on, Sally. Come on and cry," Mom said.

But Sally wasn't the least bit sad.

"I need help, honey. I can't do it alone." Mom's voice nearly broke. She clenched her parched hands.

Sally didn't want to mourn. Why should she weep just so the dumb grass could grow and puddles could fill and cows could drink and the world could be blue and cool?

Dad knocked over the lamp. Thunder whimpered in the distance.

"Sally, *please*," Mom whimpered. She was too eager to serve. Just a dishrag too soon threadbare, a gray mop-head limp from swabbing, a puckered lemon squeezed dry of juice. Sally grew more angry than sad when thinking of Mom's years of sacrifice.

Dad put a boot through the sheetrock wall and lightning flashed and thunder split the sky. Sally wanted to be like him and bring the thunder. That was braver and crueler. None of these foolish tears.

Mom was behind schedule, not matching Dad's ruckus. Her weakness threw her timing off. Soon it would all be up to Sally. And that made Sally damp with rage.

She closed her eyes and thought of Mom, who was barely able to summon a good dew. Mom was failing and fading. Just as Sally would be in twenty-five years. And with that realization, the tears came, slowly at first, then faster.

Drops rattled off the roof and Sally looked out the window. Through her tears she saw streaks of silver-gray, the small diamond drops bouncing and breaking on the earth, the ground drinking the gift she had made. Mom had stopped trying to cry, only sat and watched with a pleased smile, proud to have a daughter who was her spitting image.

Sally cried rhythmically and easily now that the clouds

had burst. Dad stormed up a storm and rumbled his rage and the sky echoed his anguish. Sally cried until she was weary from weeping. Rain fell and the plains refreshed themselves, pricked up its corn, stiffened its marigolds and shivered its thick trees.

Then the wind person must have grown tired of puffing and blowing, because the clouds broke apart and spread out like wool jam on gray bread. Dad fell on the couch, exhausted, the summer heat of effort making his forehead bead with sweat.

Sally sniffed and blinked. She dried her eyes with the corner of the tablecloth. At least Mom hadn't sliced onions, as she had done last week when Sally's tears refused to fall.

Outside, the sun came, and the last drips fell from the rusty gutter onto the porch. The air was scrubbed clean, its molecules full of fresh green, smelling of renewed life. Dad returned to the couch.

"Good job, honey," Mom said, patting Sally's hand. "I'm afraid I'm just not much help these days."

"Why do you keep on, then? Why can't—"

"— someone else do it? There *is* no one else, at least in this part of the country. Only me. And now you, dear."

"But it's not fair. Making the rain is hard work. Melanie Higgins doesn't have to do it. Vince and Selena don't have to worry about crying when the sky needs them. And Jason—"

"But you're not like them."

"Why not?"

Mom shrugged. "The world needs rain. We bring it. Who are we to know the reason for such things?"

"Could be worse." Dad had opened the paper again and spoke from behind the rumpled pages. "Them in the Sahara, the Mojave, the Painted Desert, the Gobi, places were the rain people died out, them folks are suffering. We ain't so bad off here. We got shade trees and a roof over our heads."

"But—"

"No more buts, ifs, or druthers, young lady," Dad said, dipping the newspaper to send his stormy glare at Sally. "You'll do as your mother says."

"But I want to be like everybody else." Sally stood and stamped her foot. "I won't be a rain girl for the rest of my life. *I won't, I won't, I WON'T.*"

Sally ran to her room and threw herself on the bed. She put her head under the pillow and sobbed. The rain started again, mad on the windowsill. It poured until Mom came in an hour later to soothe her.

"What do you want to do?"

"I don't know. What do you want to do?"

What Sally really wanted to do was exactly what they were doing now. Nothing.

Jason skipped a rock across the creek, a four-hopper. He looked coolly at the sky, at the fat orange gob of sun sinking toward September. Sally watched him. She liked to watch him.

He had blue eyes and a flame of hair, and his shoulders were starting to broaden. His voice was deeper than those of the other boys on the block. He was different, better than the others.

They sat on the smooth black rocks and watched a crawdad make a milky mud-trail on the bottom of the creek. The shade was pleasant. The high trees fanned them. Or maybe one of the wind people was breathing hard.

"School starts in a few weeks."

"Yeah," Sally said. "Where has summer gone?"

"Where did it even come from?"

Sally looked at him closely. Did he *know*? Or was he just guessing? She decided he was just making strange talk. He couldn't know about the season people, about the tug-of-war between the spring folks and the summer hotheads, the nerveless winterers and the brown brittle autumn makers. Ordinary people didn't know the true workings of nature.

Sally hugged her knees to her chest. *Jason, eyes of ice,* she thought. *You should be a winter boy. Because your eyes are cold and blue and you see the end of things.*

But she said nothing, only listened to the music that some creek minder was playing, a tinkle here, a glug and gurgle there, a soft swallowing splash and a fishy laugh.

Jason was tossing a mudball in the air, spinning it in his quick hands.

"Seventh grade next year. That means we'll have Miss Fenwick. It's going to be a long year." Jason's head bobbed as he followed the path of the mudball.

"She's not so bad," Sally said. They sat in the long shadow of evening for a while without speaking.

"Jason?"

"Hmm?"

"Is Melanie going to be your girl next year?"

The mudball stopped, held in one hand. "Melanie?"

"I saw you kissing her on the playground last spring."

The mudball started again, more slowly. "That was just kissing. I don't want Melanie to be my girl."

"But Melanie says—"

"Melanie says a lot of things."

Another silence, shorter this time, and the gap was filled with the first night noises as the man who tucked in the sun started his daily labors. The insect conductor lifted her arms somewhere, counting out the beats with a dandelion wand.

Crickets and late birds played their notes, and a beagle across the meadow flubbed its lines.

Sally's heart was beating fast, like Dad's during a thunderstorm. "Are you going to you...you know— have a girl?"

"Been thinking about it."

The mudball landed in the black water of the creek. Jason moved from his rock to sit beside Sally. The stone cooled beneath them.

"Been thinking, maybe you. If you want to, that is." Jason's breath was close, an odd whispering wind, warm but fresh on her cheek, followed by lips on hers, all as mysterious as night.

Sally skipped into the living room, whistling.

"You've been chipper lately," Mom said.

"It's autumn. I don't have to do those stupid afternoon rains anymore."

Mom put her hands on her hips. "Now, I can tell it's more than that. I was a girl once, too."

Sally found that hard to imagine, looking at Mom now. A thousand years of sorrow were etched on her forehead. "Well, anyway, thunderstorm season is over."

"It's been weeks since a rain, though. I think we'll need one later this evening. Getting a little dusty outside."

That evening, Dad pitched his usual fit. Sally tried to squeeze some tears out of the corners of her eye, but it was no use. Her heart was too light, a helium balloon, a seagull, pink cotton candy.

Mom sliced two onions. No good. Thunder shook the windowpanes, but the sky kept its bottom and hoarded its liquid jewels.

Weeks passed. School had started, the fields withered,

dwarf corn shriveled, peas rattled in their pods, oldtimers leaned on fences and recollected the great droughts of their youth.

Sally tried every night, tried to be sad, tried to weep. She sniffed onions and thought of sick puppies and broken toys and funerals and other sorrowful things. Once she even poked herself in the eye. Still the fields lay dry and aching.

She saw Jason every day at school, and they walked holding hands every afternoon, kissing by the creek when the other children weren't around. The creek was thinner now, weak between the smooth stones, quieter and less merry. The sky was cloudless.

The autumn makers rolled out golden rugs, applied their red and orange brushstrokes, underpinned the landscape with brown. The trees thirsted and gave up their leaves too soon. The ground cracked and sighed. Still no rain.

October came, on dried batwings.

The Halloween dance was coming up at school. Sally sat at her desk, excited by the chaff in the air and that sweet melancholy aroma the grass gave off just before the winter women put it to sleep. Sally cut her paper pumpkins and bundled her corn by its bleached husks. She wanted a drink of water, but the school principal had shut off the fountain because of the water shortage.

Sally didn't feel guilty. So what if the pumpkins were shrunken and scarecrows withered at their posts? She had tried to rain. It wasn't her fault that all those stupid people shook their fists at the sky and sent up airplanes with silver iodide and cast their hopeful doomed eyes at each occasional cloud. She hadn't asked to be a rain girl, anyway.

Classes were dismissed early for the holiday, but Sally stayed to finish the decorations that would hang in the gym on twisted orange and black streamers. She stood to stretch her legs. Her fingers were sore from scissoring. But she didn't mind. Tonight she would be dancing with Jason.

She walked down the hall on the pillows of daydreams. She had a new dress to wear, one her mother had made as Sally sat at the table each evening and tried to drum some rain. Mom had worked the needle and kept looking up at Sally, her eyes red and dry and hollow. Dad had cursed, but only managed to summon some heat lightning.

Sally opened the school door. Even the sunshine didn't bother her. She thought of the dress that was waiting at home. It was blue, the color of a mean sky, and she couldn't wait to wear it. Even Melanie never had a dress like it.

Four steps across crisp grass.

Shapes over by the swingset.

Somewhere, the wind people gasped.

Jason was kissing Melanie.

Sally stared, disbelieving.

The shapes blurred, shimmered in her damp eyes.

"Sally, wait," Jason called. Melanie laughed.

Sally ran toward home without looking back.

The sky opened its throat, empty of clouds but spewing a silent silver grief. Her heart was as leaden as the air. Her drenched clothes clung to her like a second skin.

She found home and bed and Mom, but still the ache tore at her heart.

"What's wrong, honey?" Mom said, sitting on the bed. Beneath the concern in Mom's voice, Sally heard elation and relief. Rain pounded on the shingles, steady and untiring and passionate. Puddles stretched themselves outward and rivers swelled with Sally's hurt. Shriveled apples were knocked from their branches and umbrellas collapsed like tissues.

Ordinary people watched from their windows as the sudden rain fell. Minutes before, not a cloud had dotted the sky. But in the people's happiness they forgot all about the oddness of it, too joyful that the dry spell was broken. They stuck out their tongues and quenched themselves.

The rain kept on into the night and throughout the next day, soaking all the kids who went to the Halloween dance. Then two more days without pause, the ground saturated and the ditches swollen, brown water churning over sewer grates, all pulled by the gravity girl toward the far gulf. The creeks bloated, and the creek minders wrung their hands, flustered by the loss of control.

On the fourth day, when the rivers leapt their banks and people evacuated their front porches in rowboats, when everyone huddled in yellow slickers and no dry socks remained, then, then, they started worrying.

Young hearts are slow in healing.

Sally drowned November.

Do You Know Me Yet?

It all started with a story. You know the one I mean, don't you, Doctor?

Of course you do. You know everything. You smile and nod and write down little words on your paper and then go home at the end of the day, safe in the knowledge that I'm the crazy one and you're normal.

But let me tell you something. These walls work both ways. They not only keep people in, they keep you "normal" people out. Except you have a key, don't you? You can come and go anytime you want. Just like my ideas. They come and go anytime I want them to.

I know what you just wrote. "Episodic paranoia?" With a question mark. Where's your smile now, doctor? Try to hide it under that bald head of yours, it won't do any good. I can read thoughts. That's why I'm here. That's why *they* put me here.

Except they're the crazy ones. See, they can read thoughts, too. Only they do it better than me. And the world calls them "leading lights" and "visionaries," the critics rave about how they "stare unflinchingly into the darkness." The editors fight over them, make fools of themselves in their rush to outbid each other. Agents snap like sharks in a bloody sea, hoping to get a piece.

Sorry. I'm getting angry, and my last doctor told me that getting angry is not the path to healing. And I want to be cured. I really do. I want to get outside again. They won't let me have any pencils or pens or other sharp objects, and it's really hard to write novels with crayons. Plus editors won't look at handwritten manuscripts.

Tell about how it started? Again? How many years did you go to school to earn a piece of paper that empowers you to judge me? Ten years of college, just like I thought. Seems like you'd need a good memory to get through all those classes.

But I'll do it. Because I'm a storyteller, and you're the audience. Even if I can read your thoughts and know that you don't believe a word of what I say. At least you're honest, and by that, I mean you don't lie to my face. Not like *them*.

It started way back then, with my story about the girl with psychokinesis. You don't believe in psychokinesis. But that's okay. It's not what you believe that matters. It's what I believe, and what I know.

I wrote that story in the early 1970's. Well, actually, I didn't get to write it. But I thought about it almost every day for two years. This girl is in high school, see, and all her classmates pick on her because she's so weird. Her mom's a religious zealot, and the girl doesn't have anybody to turn to when her mental powers start developing. PK always comes on with adolescence, see?

I never figured out how it was going to end, but I really was going to start writing. I bought a Royal typewriter and a bunch of paper. You can look it up, it's all in that civil suit I brought against that creep who stole my story. I can't mention his name, because of legal reasons, but one day the truth will come out.

So anyway, imagine my anger when that story came out as a bestseller in paperback, movie rights sold, and that low-down dirty thief quit his day job and became an overnight success. Sure, his agent put this spin on later, about how the guy wrote six hours a day for fifteen years, about how he'd been submitting stories since he was twelve or so, and that he'd been publishing short stories in naughty magazines. But you know the lengths they go to when they have to cover their tracks. And everybody knows they got the millions. Millions that should be mine.

Ah, you just crossed out the question mark, didn't you? "Episodic paranoia." No doubt about it, in your mind. You're smug, Doctor. As smug as they are. Everybody's right, and I'm wrong.

Go on? Sure, I'll go on. See, I'm controlling my temper. Just like the last doctor told me to do. And you're thinking that if you let me talk, I'll calm down and you can be done with me in time for your five o'clock martini. See me smile.

Back before I was a writer, when I was just a kid, I had this other idea. About a woman who has the Devil's baby. When the book came out about that one, I just figured it was a coincidence. But then when that guy stole my idea about the little girl who gets possessed by Satan and a Catholic priest tries to save her, I decided I'd better become a writer, too. I figured that if my ideas were so good that other people wanted to steal them, I'd better write them myself. That's when I came up with the psychokinesis idea.

Have I ever written anything? Sure, I have. I get a good sentence or two down, and then I stare at the paper. It's called "writer's block," and only creative people get it. That's why you breeze right through those papers you submit to the trade journals. That's the reason all these other writers are so prolific. It's easy when somebody else is doing your thinking for you.

Well, I decided I'd hurry through my next couple of books before somebody could steal my ideas. Except that one guy types faster than I do. So he beat me to the one about the virus that wipes out most of the world so God and the Devil can fight over the survivors, and he beat me to the one about the haunted hotel. And get this...

Whenever I got writer's block, do you know what I used to type? "All work and no play makes Jack a dull boy." And you-know-who steals it and everybody thinks it's the most clever thing to ever grace a page. And they call *me* crazy.

His best trick was when he "released" all these books that he'd supposedly written before he got famous. I had all of those ideas in one night, right after the PK book came out. You know, the walking race where only the winner survives, the same idea again except this time it's set in the future and the competitors are paid to run for their lives, one where a man blows up stuff because he doesn't like progress, and one where a kid shoots up his high school. That last one was so dumb I didn't think anybody would steal it. But you-know-who types a lot faster than he thinks, so he'd probably mailed it to his publisher before he realized what it was about.

And he was clever, because he knew I was on to him. He even came up with a pen name for those books so that I would have to sue him twice. I guess he figured I couldn't afford lawyers' fees. I was just a poor writer, see? Never mind that I'd never actually published anything.

It was bad enough when only a few people were picking my brain. Once in a while, I could feel them, up there in my skull, tiptoeing around and fighting each other for the best ideas. But then people across the ocean got into the act. People in England and some people who couldn't even speak English. That's what I call power, when your ideas are so universal that they cross lingual and cultural barriers. But my head was getting crowded.

Ah, you just crossed out a word. Now it's just "paranoia." And you're about to write "delusions of grandeur." Why do they let you have a pencil and not me?

We both know why, don't we? Because then I would write down my ideas before they could steal them. The hospital's in on it, too. Yes, you can smile about it, like you've got a secret. But we both know better.

Let's see, where were we? Because you are my audience and I don't want to lose you.

Oh, yes. My idea about a bunch of old men who had fallen in love with a ghost a long time ago. A different writer got that one. But instead of getting mad, I became more determined than ever. I quit my job and did nothing but think all the time, getting wonderful ideas one after another. Psychic vampires, sympathetic vampires who are more romantic than scary, a killer clown that's really a UFO buried under the ground, a puzzle box that opens another dimension, giant rats that live in the sewer system, paranormal investigators who discover a haunted town, a child that's really the Antichrist, so many ideas I could hardly keep track.

Everyone was stealing from me. Even writers who could barely make out a shopping list. Only the critics called it the "horror boom," and you couldn't pass the paperback rack in the supermarket without an army of foil-covered monsters grinning out at you. My monsters. Some I wasn't too proud of, but they're like children. You still have to love them, even the dumb and ugly ones.

I just kept getting ideas, and they kept stealing them. They got richer while I got madder. And I mean "mad" in the real way, not in the crazy way. But the maddest I ever got was when that British writer pulled a satire on me.

See, he wrote this story you may have read. Called it "Next Time You'll Know Me." I know the story, and I've never even read it. Because I met him at a convention, and as I was shaking his hand, I was thinking that I hoped he didn't steal any of my ideas, because then I'd have to get him, and he seemed like such a nice fellow.

Of course, I'd never get him in real life, because only crazy people do things like that. But he looked at me, and he had a twinkle in his eye, and he started writing the story right there in his head. *My* story! About how a pyscho thinks writers are stealing his ideas. I was going to say something, to claim copyright infringement, but the next woman in line pushed me away so she could shake the famous writer's hand.

Ever wonder where ideas come from? No, I suppose not. You don't have very much imagination. I guess you can't afford to, in your line of work.

Well, see, I wondered about where ideas came from, after that British writer made me so mad. And it took me years of thinking about it before I realized that ideas came from *me*. So I made myself stop getting them, so the other writers couldn't steal them.

Of course, some great ideas still slip out once in a while. I can't shut down such a wondrous force all the time. So you-know-who manages to steal two or three per year, and a few others are still getting their share. But the "horror boom" faded, and if you'll notice, publishers are avoiding horror books right now because I stopped letting my good ideas loose.

Shutting down wasn't easy for a writer like me, who loves ideas more than the actual writing. It was hard work, and gave me a headache. That, and the stress of all those lawsuits I filed against the thieves. That's why I did all those bad things that put me behind these walls. Or in front of them, depending on how you look at it.

Why is it I had ideas for only *horror* stories? Leave it to a shrink to ask something like that. Oh, you'll really going to have a field day with that, aren't you? Well, ideas just come, and you can't do anything about them. Unless you're me.

I know you're going to look in your diagnostic manual tonight and come up with some long explanation of why you think I'm crazy. Except you don't call it "crazy," do you? These are kinder, gentler times. You have to call it a "behavioral disorder."

I don't care what label you attach to me. I don't believe in psychology. I don't believe in insanity. I don't believe in shrinks.

Oh, you're offended? Well, let me fill you in on a little secret, because you're not as good at reading minds as your predecessor. Did the hospital tell you why he resigned? Of course not. All you shrinks keep your secrets, even from each other.

Well, I'll tell you why he left. We were sitting here, just like you and I are doing, and I was telling him my story. And all of a sudden I got this great idea for a novel. It just slipped out before I even realized what I was thinking about. And it's a doozy. I may as well tell you about it, because it's too late for you to steal it. Plus, no offense, but I don't think you have what it takes to be a real writer like me.

Okay, the idea. This guy is in the psychiatric ward because he thinks people are stealing his ideas. Only nobody believes him, and they all think he's crazy. So he escapes, and goes out to get revenge on all the writers who have made millions off of his ideas. Only when he gets out in the real world, he finds out that he's really just an *idea*, that he doesn't even exist at all. So it's like he's a ghost, which makes it real easy to get to these famous writers.

But the hero is smart, he doesn't kill them or anything. That would be too easy. And they would be famous forever, and readers and critics would never know the lie behind the success stories. So the hero gives the writers *bad* ideas, sneaks in at night and alters their manuscripts, gives them a mild enough case of writer's block that they get desperate. I thought about calling the book "Desperation," but that one guy is so good he steals my titles before I even come up with them.

Pretty good idea, huh? Well, the doctor snatched it right out of my head, and if you pick up the latest *Publisher's Weekly*, you'll see that he just got a six-figure advance on an outline and sample chapter. It can happen to anybody, if you get a good idea. If you steal them from me.

See how well I'm controlling my anger? I'll bet *you* wouldn't be so calm, if you were in my shoes. But I'm used to it by now. I'm the idea man. I could almost be happy with that, and accept my place in the literary landscape. But the thing that bugs me the most is that *nobody else* knows. I'm not getting any credit.

And there's one more thing. I'm a writer. And some day I'm going to get around to actually writing. One day soon, you're going to let me have a pencil and some paper, maybe even a typewriter after I prove I'm not a threat to myself or others.

And I will write down my ideas, all the ones I kept

locked away all these years. I have a lot of them. I'm going to be rich. Nobody thinks you're crazy when you're rich, even if you're a horror writer.

And after I'm cured, when you think about what I've said and realize I'm right, you're going to rubber-stamp my papers and I will be on the outside again. I know, I said a while ago that walls work both ways, but that was crazy talk, and you can see that I'm no longer crazy. You are such a good doctor that you are curing me. I'm feeling much better.

No, if I get out, I certainly won't go after all those writers who got rich off of my ideas. That would be acting paranoid. Anyway, I'll be too busy writing down my new ideas, which will be much better than the old ones. In fact, the readers will forget about all those other writers.

So that will be my revenge. I'll knock them off the bestseller lists. And I'll let them have only my worst ideas. I'll make millions, and the critics will eat those "ooh-la-lahs" alive.

Oh, I may do one more thing. After you let me out, I'm going to fly to the Merseyside. I'm going to hunt down that writer who satired me. I'm not going to stalk him or anything, and I won't be carrying any sharp objects, except maybe a writing pen.

Maybe I'll come up to him in a grocery store, or at a bus stop, or in a dark pub. I'll look him in the eye and see if it twinkles. I'll say, "Do you know me yet?"

And I'll wait for him to ask for my autograph.

See me smile.

Homecoming

The wind cut through the valley like a frozen razor. Black clouds raced from the west, shrouding the setting sun. Leaves skittered over the brown grass. The air smelled of electricity and rust and dried chestnut and things long dead.

No ghosts flickered among the sagging fence posts outside, no spirits swept over the hay-strewn barnyard. Only earthly shadows moved in the twilight, nothing but swaying trees and nightbirds and loose gates. Charlie Roniger turned from the dark glass of the window.

"It's gonna come a storm," he said, drawing the dusty curtains. His wife, Sara, sat in her ragged easy chair and said nothing. She looked deeply into the flames crackling in the fireplace. Her wrinkled hands were folded over the quilt in her lap, hands that had once snapped green beans and wrung out wet sheets and caressed the soft down on a baby's head.

Charlie studied her face. It was fallen, as if the framework behind it was busted up like an old hatbox. He never thought she'd end up broken. Not the way she'd always been able to show her feelings, to hold the family together, to love the only two men in her life.

She was too much like that old spring up on the hill, just kept on slow and steady until you came to expect it to run on forever. Then when it dried up, you got mad, even though you had no promise that it would keep running. Even when you knew you had no real right to it. It was a blessing, and blessings weren't made to last. Otherwise, the bad things that God sent along wouldn't get their proper due.

Charlie reached into the front pocket of his denim overalls and pulled out a plug of tobacco. He twisted off a chaw with his three good teeth. His gums mashed the tobacco until it was moist and pliable. Then, with his tongue, he pushed the wad into the hollow of his jaw.

He walked to the door, unconsciously checking the lock. On a peg beside his overcoat hung the baseball glove he'd given Johnny for his tenth birthday. The leather had shrunk and cracked from all the years Johnny had lobbed dewy walnuts on the tin roof of the barn, pretending he was catching fly balls off Yankee bats. Johnny had been a southpaw. He'd gotten that from Sara's side of the family.

Charlie wished he'd had more time to play catch with his son. But the fields always needed his plow, the hay had to be pressed into yellow squares, the hogs squealed for slop, the corn cried for water. The forest gave its trees but demanded in trade hours of stretched muscles and stinging sweat. Even the soil begged for his flesh, whispering to him to lie down and rot and feed the new roots.

So time went away, the sun rose and fell like a rib cage drawing in deep breaths. And chores and meals and church on Sundays stole the years. Charlie wondered if all you were left with at the end was the memory of all the things you should have said but never could. Things like "I love you."

He touched the glove that was as rough and parched as his own skin. He always thought it would be the other way around, with him fading out slow and gaspy and full of pain while Johnny stood over the bed and tried to get up the nerve to hug him. And Charlie thought he might have been able to say it then, when they were both scared and had nothing to lose. Back when death looked like a one-way road.

Charlie stooped, his spine popping as he reached into the firebox and grabbed a couple of oak logs with his arthritic fingers. He carried the wood into the living room and tossed them onto the fire, sending a shower of sparks up the chimney. The reflection of the fire danced in his wife's glassy eyes, red-orange pinpricks on bald onyx. She didn't blink.

"Fire feels good, don't it, honey?" he said gently, squirting a stream of brown juice into the flames. The liquid hissed and evaporated as he waited for an answer, knowing it wouldn't come. Language had left her alone, even if the dead folks hadn't.

Outside, the wind picked up. The old two-story house creaked and leaned against the coming gale. A few loose shingles flapped, and the upstairs windows rattled. Blasts of cold air swirled under the front door and the first raindrops spattered the porch.

Charlie gingerly led Sara up the squeaky stairs to bed and tucked her under the thick blankets. He checked the weather once more, but all he could see was black and his own reflection. He tossed on a back log, spit out his chaw, and locked the door. He went upstairs to wait for them.

He fell asleep with his arm around Sara, nuzzling into the hard edges of her bones. The howling wind came into his dreams and turned into a familiar moan. He awoke in a sweat and blinked into the blackness around him. Faint blue-white shapes hovered above the bed. He reached for his wife, but felt only the cool sheets in the little hollow of the bed where she should have been.

She was with them, dancing and waving her frail arms, as she had every night since Johnny had been buried. The translucent wisps flowed over her, caressing her skin and weaving around her worn flannel nightgown. She floated two feet off the ground, embraced by the spirits. They were all locked together in a hoe-down of resurrection.

As Charlie's eyes adjusted, he could make out the feathery shapes taking form. It was the regulars, the happy hour crowd of the dead set. The ghosts filled the room like joyful clouds. They cavorted like they had time to kill and forever to do it in.

Familiar faces coalesced among the mists. There was Doris, the school teacher, who had passed on in the winter of '73, now as withered as a forgotten houseplant. Freddie, Charlie's old fishing buddy, was moaning and hooting like an eviscerated owl. He had drowned several years ago and his skin was stretched and pale like a bleached water balloon. Freddie had lost his hat, and Charlie noticed for the first time how large his ears were.

Colonel Hadley was hovering like a shroud on a coat hanger, wearing his military dress blues even though his ramrod days were over. The town gossip held that Fanny Coffey had run off with a traveling Bible salesman, but she couldn't have made it far on those amputated legs. The Bible salesman had answered a newfound calling to be a sex murderer, an about-face career change that caught Fanny by surprise. Consumptive old Pete Henries fumbled at his chest, aimlessly searching for another of the cigarettes that had nailed his coffin lid shut. The Waters bunch looked on, father and mother and child, still as ashen as they had been on the morning they were found in their garage with the Buick engine running.

Rhetta Mae Harper was among them, Rhetta Mae who had tried to seduce Charlie when Sara had been so knotted up with pregnancy that she couldn't bear her husband's touch. Sara's womb had taken his seed in late middle age, and the fetus that would be Johnny kept her in constant discomfort. Charlie had tasted Rhetta Mae's temptation and had nearly swallowed, but in the end his love for Sara kept him true. Rhetta Mae had been shot during some drunken, jealous frenzy, her voluptuous figure shredded by number eight buckshot pellets. Charlie found her charms much easier to resist now.

He kicked off the blankets and rolled out of the old cast-iron bed, the mattress springs and his bones creaking in harmony. The cold pine floorboards chilled his feet as he walked over to his wife. The ghosts crowded Charlie's face, but he brushed them aside like cobwebs. He put his hand on Sara's arm. She tried feebly to fight him off. She wanted to play with her see-through friends.

"Johnny isn't here," Charlie said to Sara. "They won't take you to Johnny."

She tried to answer but could only gurgle like an infant. She was finding ecstasy in those icy arms.

"Now get the hell outta here, you bunch of deadbeats," Charlie shouted at the ghosts, trembling with chill and outrage. For some reason he didn't understand, they always obeyed him, as if they hadn't a will of their own and took their masters where they found them.

The ghosts turned to him, blank faces drooping, like children who had been scolded for taking baby chicks out of a nest. They gently lowered Sara and she stood on the wobbly sticks of her legs. The figures flitted into shadows and disappeared.

The storm had blown over now and a sliver of moonlight spilled across the bedroom. Charlie laid his wife down
and tugged the blankets over her. He got in beside her and
watched the corners of the room. Johnny's photograph was
on the dresser, the portrait grinning in the weak moonlight.
Smooth skin and a proud shy smile, those eyes that Sara said
were so much like his father's. *Damn shame about that boy*, he
thought, as his rage faded like the ghosts had. Sorrow rose
from a shallow grave in his heart to take its place.

They said Johnny had slipped down at the sawmill, his
flannel sleeve yanked by the hungry blade that didn't discrimi-
nate between limbs of poplar, jack pine, or flesh. The lumber
company sent a check and paid for his funeral. It rained the
day they lowered Johnny's purple casket into the ground. Rivulets of red streaked the clay as the gravediggers shoveled.
Charlie thought it was funny how they threw in that coffin
and all that dirt, and the hole still wasn't full. He and Sara
watched the rain drill down into the man-sized puddle long
after the minister had fled for the shelter of his powder-blue
Cadillac.

The ghosts had paid their first visit that night. Sara's
mind, already splintered by grief, took a final wrong turn down
the dirt road of madness. Charlie had been disbelieving at first,
but now the midnight stops were another part of the day, as
fixed in the rhythm of his life as milking the cows and gather-
ing the eggs. Just another hardship to be endured.

Charlie turned his eyes from the photograph and
reached for the tobacco. Since he was awake, he might as well
have a chaw. He rested his wiry neck back on the pillow and
worked the sticky sweet leaf with his gums. Something rustled
by the dresser.

"You're a little late, the show's over," Charlie said. The noise continued.

Charlie raised his head and saw a faint apparition trying to form by the closet. *Damned if it ain't a new one,* he thought. Threads of milky air spun themselves into a human shape. Charlie blinked and looked at the photograph.

"Can't be," he muttered. Then he realized it was the one he'd been waiting for, night after long night. "Johnny? Is that you, boy?"

A voice like December answered, "Yeah, Dad."

Charlie sat up in bed, his heart pounding. He glanced sideways at his wife. Her eyes were closed, and the blankets rose and fell with her even breathing.

"How's it going, son?"

"Not too bad. I've been a little confused here lately."

"Didn't I tell you to keep an eye out for that damned sawblade? Just look what you've gone and done to yourself."

Johnny materialized more fully and stepped forward into the moonlight. Flesh hung in ropes from his ruined cheeks. His nose was missing, and chunks of his hair had been torn from his savaged scalp. His Adam's apple bobbed uncontrollably, dangling by a tendon from the gash in his neck.

Charlie gulped, feeling the tobacco sting his throat. "You're looking real good, son."

"How's Mom?"

"She's fine," Charlie said. "We better let her sleep, though. Her spring's dried up."

Johnny nodded as if that made sense. The Adam's apple quivered and made a wet sound.

"They took your pitching arm, son. That was supposed to win you a college scholarship."

Johnny contemplated his missing left hand as if he could

still see it. "It happened so fast, Dad. Hurt for a second, like when you get rope burns or something, but then it was over. Seems like only yesterday, but seems like it never happened, too. Lots of things are funny that way lately."

Charlie looked into Johnny's eyes that were deep as graves. He suddenly remembered teaching his son how to tie a slip-knot on a fishing line. They had stood in the shade of a sycamore, where the branches were highest, so the hooks wouldn't snag. Johnny's stubby fingers had fumbled with the line as his face clenched in determination, but now the fingers of his remaining hand were ragged and moldy, with dirt packed under the nails.

Charlie felt the blankets slip from his shoulders, and a coldness flooded his chest as if his heart had frozen. "You feel like talking about it, son?"

"Well, I'm supposed to be looking for something. I thought I ought to come here," Johnny said, the bone of his head slowly swiveling.

"Home is where you go when you got trouble," Charlie said. "I told you I'd always be here to help you."

"Dad, it ain't the hurt, 'cause I don't feel nothing. But I'm lost, like. Can't seem to find my way."

Charlie gummed his chaw quickly and nervously before answering. "You know you'd be welcome here, but I don't think that's right. There's others that are your kind now."

"I reckon so," Johnny said softly, looking at and through his own torso as if finally understanding. Then his hollow voice lifted. "You remember when those Corcoran boys were picking on me, and you stared down their whole damned brood? Walked right up on their front porch, standing on them old boards ready to fight 'em one at a time or all at once. That sure took the steam out of their britches."

"Nobody messes with my boy." Charlie looked into the shadows that passed for Johnny's eyes.

"Say, Dad, whatever happened to Darlene?"

Charlie didn't want Johnny to rest any less easily than he already did. He couldn't say that Darlene had married Jack Corcoran when Johnny was barely six weeks in the ground, before the grass even had time to take root over his grave. Fond memories might give the dead comfort, for all Charlie knew. So he lied.

"She pined and pined, boy. Broke her poor little heart. But eventually she got on with her life, the way a body does. That would have made one fine wedding, you and her."

"I only wanted to make her happy. And you, too, Dad. I guess I'll never get the chance now."

The dark maw in the center of Johnny's face gaped like an endless wet cave.

"We all got our own row to hoe, Johnny. I taught you that we take care of our own. But I also told you that you gotta make hard choices along the way. And it looks like this is one path that you better walk alone."

Johnny shuffled his shredded feet. "Yeah, I reckon so. But I ain't scared. I guess it's what ought to be."

Charlie felt a stirring in the blankets beside him.

"Them other ones been here lookin' for you. Been here ever damn night, bugging hell out of your mom," Charlie said quickly.

Sara sat up, her eyes moist with sleep. She gasped as she saw the scraps of her son. Charlie put a hand on her shoulder to keep her from getting out of bed.

A thin strand of drool ran down her chin as she tried to speak. "Juhhhnn..."

Johnny drifted forward. "Mom?"

Charlie pressed Sara's head down onto her pillow. "You'd best be getting on, son. No need to stir up trouble here."

Johnny moved closer, though not one of his limbs moved. He was beside the bed now, and Charlie felt the stale cold draft of his son's deathwind. Johnny reached out with a hand that was the color of a trout belly.

Sara squirmed under Charlie's arm, but Charlie pinned her and pulled the quilt over her face. When he looked back at Johnny, the vacant expression had been replaced by a look that Charlie had seen one other time. A possum had crawled under the henhouse wire, and Charlie went after it with a pitchfork when the animal refused to give up its newfound territory. Charlie must have jabbed the possum fifty or sixty times, with it hissing and snarling every breath right up until it finally died.

Charlie wondered what kind of pitchfork you used on a ghost.

The mottled hand came closer, and Charlie clenched his teeth. "Ain't proper for a grown man to be making his mother cry."

Johnny paused for a moment, and his eyes looked like they were filled with muddy water.

"That's right," Charlie said. "You're springs drying up. You got other rivers to run to, now."

Sara kicked Charlie's leg, but he wasn't about to turn her loose.

Johnny reached out and touched Charlie's cheek. His son's fingers were like icicles. The hand trailed along the line of Charlie's stubble, as if remembering the scratchiness he'd felt against his infant skin. It was the first time they had touched in nearly twenty years.

"I'd best go with them. Seems only right," Johnny whispered in his lost voice. Affection and a strange pride fluttered in Charlie's chest. This was his only son standing before him. Did it matter that his decaying guts were straining against the cotton of his burial shirt? As a father, it was his duty to teach his son one more of life's harsh little lessons.

"A man's gotta do what a man's gotta do." Charlie pointed to the far corner of the room. "They went that-a-ways."

Johnny turned his mutilated face, a face that only a mother could love. Then he looked back. He leaned over Charlie and spread his arms wide. The raw meat of his throat jogged as he spoke. "I love you, Dad."

Without thinking, Charlie reached up, his hands passing through the moist silk of Johnny's flesh. But how could you hug a dried-up spring? How could you hug a memory?

Charlie loved the son who had walked this earth. The small boy who had sat between Charlie's legs on the tractor, pretending to steer while making engine noises with his mouth. The son he had taken to see the Royals play, who had built an awkward birdhouse in eighth-grade shop for his mother, who had slept in the hayloft in the summer because he liked the smell. The son who had buried his old hound himself because he didn't want anyone to see him cry. Johnny did those things, not this blasphemy hovering over him.

Johnny had been the flesh of Charlie's flesh, but this thing was beyond flesh. Resting in peace was a comfort for the living, not the dead.

He almost said the words anyway. But he found he'd rather take his regrets to the grave. Second chances be damned.

"It's good to see you, son." Like hell.

"Tell Mom that I miss her." Johnny's maw opened and closed raggedly. Sara was sobbing under the blankets, her fragile bones trembling.

"I will. You take care, now." Like he was sending

Johnny off to summer Bible camp.

Johnny shimmered and faded, the dutiful son to the last. His stump of a left arm raised as if to wave good-bye. The essence that had been Charlie's only son fluttered and vanished just as the first rays of dawn broke through the room. The ghosts wouldn't be back. They had what they had been looking for.

Charlie relaxed and pulled the blankets off his wife's face. She turned her back to him, her gray hair matted against the pillowcase. He touched her shoulder but she shrugged him away. Something rattled in her chest.

He rose from the bed and dressed, working the tightness out of his stringy muscles. He rubbed his hands together to drive away the lingering chill of his son's touch. His heart felt like a charred ember in the ash of a dead fire. His eyes burned, but they had always been miserly when it came to making tears.

He knew you couldn't expect it to keep running forever. When the spring dries up, you had to remember that you had no promise that it would keep on. The water's for everybody or even nobody at all. You had no real right to it in the first place.

Charlie stopped by the front door and put on his overcoat and heavy work gloves. Firewood was waiting outside, frosty and unsplit. He took his ax and his loving memories out under the morning sun so he could hold them to the light.

Kill Your Darlings

I was wiping down the counter with an old shirt rag when he came in. The man in the yellow slicker. I saw him without looking up, drank him in the way my customers downed their Scotch and water. Years of bartending had made me a quick study. Call it survival instinct.

Big guy, woolly Groucho Marx eyebrows, but his nose was small and sharp, more like a hawk's bill than an eagle's beak. He was an easy 6'2" if he was an inch, and he was at least an inch. He was slouching down into the collar of his slicker, trying to make himself invisible. Fat chance.

He shook off the afternoon rain that had collected on his broad shoulders. Even in the dim light of neon beer signs, I could see his black smoldering eyes roaming over the joint. He wasn't here for the atmosphere, though we had plenty of that. A television in the corner, tuned to a 24-hour sports station, the sound turned down. A row of ragged barstools, their cotton stuffing oozing out from under the vinyl seats. A jukebox by the restrooms, broken down and so old that it featured "The Brand New Hit from Hank Williams!" A couple of regulars slouched in a booth, deep in their cups despite the early hour, whiling away the day until it was time to get down to some serious drinking. And all of that was doubled back in the long, foggy mirror that covered the wall behind the bar, the mirror that had a perfect round hole from a passionate gunshot maybe twenty years ago. He wasn't here for the scenery.

And he wasn't here for the smell. Stale urine laced with crusted vomit that never completely dried, just sort of congealed half-heartedly. The musty smell of the soggy carpet, worn down to the threads or, in places, all the way through to the rough pine planks underneath. The odor of old cigarettes which had seeped so deeply into the walls that you could kill a nicotine craving by chewing on a piece of the peeling wallpaper. And, of course, the grainy smell of every kind of imbibement known to man, at least the stuff that was under twenty bucks a bottle.

No, despite all this decadent splendor, he was here for something besides a blind date with a watered-down slug of rotgut. He was looking for someone. He walked across the floor to the chipped bar and sat down in front of me.

"What's your pleasure?" I asked, still not looking up, rubbing on a cigarette burn I had been working over for a few weeks.

"Business is my pleasure," he said, his voice husky and raw, his throat a clearinghouse for phlegm and bitterness—

"Honey, time to go to work," my wife Karen called from the kitchen. She put up with my writing, humored my foolish ambitions, and served as a whimsical sounding board for my evolving plots. She even let me use our apartment's overgrown pantry as a study. At least my new hobby kept me at home, unlike my earlier flings with surfboarding and collecting Civil war relics. My writing was fine with her, as long as the bills were paid.

I gulped down the gritty dregs of my coffee and looked at my wristwatch. "Coming, dear."

I left Marco in the middle of his story, along with the

guy with the raincoat. I thought of him as "Fred," but that would probably change to something more noble and tough, like "Roman." Yeah, Roman would work just fine. Roman would be looking for his wife, who had run off in the middle of the night with his best friend. Naw, that was too banal—

"Honey!"

"Okay, I'm really coming." I hit the "save" button on the word processor and jogged out of the study and into the kitchen and gave Karen a husbandly peck on the cheek. I turned before going out the door. "Be home this evening?"

"No, I've got to pick up Susanne after her soccer and then I've got a fundraiser meeting at the library," Karen said.

"Then I'll grab a burger on the way back in."

"No, you're going to heat up the pot roast and micro-wave some potatoes for us."

"Oh, yeah. Bye. Love you."

I was two minutes late at the magazine stand where I worked. I liked the job. From my position at the register, I had a clear view of the street, and the company was good, mostly educated people who actually relished honest differences of opinion. And it was great place for scoping out characters, finding faces that I could press into the two-dimensional world of fiction.

Henry, the store owner, gave me a little ribbing about being late, but he was never in a hurry to be relieved. I tried to picture his life outside the shop, but when my mind followed him down the street, him with a couple of newspapers tucked under his pudgy elbow, my imagination always gave out when he turned the corner. He was like a minor character who served his plot purpose and then dutifully shuffled off the page.

I restocked a few monthlies and had to rotate a couple of the afternoon editions that had just rolled off the presses. One of my favorite parts of the job was getting to smell the fresh paper and ink. I'd open a box of magazines or comic books and take a big relaxing sniff, like one of those turtlenecked actors "savoring the aroma" of a cup of expensive French roast.

To me, words on paper were magic: entire universes lined up in neat rows on the bookshelves, filled with heroes and heroines that dared to dream; fantastic voyages to the outermost edges of the cosmos or the inner depths of the mind; unthinkable horrors and profound rhapsodies; the vast revelations of consciousness, all for cover price and tax.

I was arranging the cigar showcase when Harriett Weatherspoon came in. She had parked her poodle by the door, and it pressed the black dot of its nose against the glass.

"Hello, Sil," she said, in her canary voice.

"Afternoon, Mrs. Weatherspoon. What will it be today?"

"I think I'll just browse through the bestsellers today."

"We've got the new Michele McMartin in. And probably an R.C. Adams or two. Seems like they come out every couple of months nowadays."

"Now, Sil, you know those are ghost-written. They come out of one of those prose-generating computer programs I read about in *Writer's Digest*."

"Million-sellers all. What does that say about the state of literacy today?"

"Charles Dickens is rolling over in his grave."

"Along with the ghosts of several Christmases."

Mrs. Weatherspoon bought a paperback and a couple of nature magazines and went out into the bright spring afternoon. She stopped at the door and unhitched her poodle's leash, and for a split-second, I thought she was going to hop on the little varmint and ride off into the sunset. But she wrapped the leash around her wrist and went down the sidewalk, chin-first.

I was watching her slip into the human stream when I

saw the man in the raincoat. He stood out from the crowd because the coat was canary yellow and also because the day was sunny and warm, with not a cloud above the skyline. Unexpected showers occasionally blew in off the coast, but most of the other pedestrians needed only an umbrella in their armpit for security. The raincoat-wearer was on the edge of a meaty crush at the corner, waiting for the light to change, and in the next moment he was gone.

"Canary yellow," I said to the empty store. "Good piece of detail. Roman's slicker will be canary yellow instead of just plain yellow."

I searched my memory to see if I could dredge any more fictional sludge out of the fleeting vision. He had been Roman's height, and he had a jot of black hair. Not the dark brown that most people call black. This was shoe-polish black. But I could steal no other features from him, because I had only seen him from behind.

Arriving home after work, I started warming up dinner and went into the study. I turned on the word processor and began spewing words, with my tongue pressed lightly between my teeth the way it does when I'm onto something and I forgot where I am, when I get sucked into a world that is trying to create itself before my eyes.

"Business is my pleasure," he said, his voice a clearinghouse for phlegm and bitterness. I hadn't heard that corny line in a few months, but I wasn't about to bring up his lack of originality.

I looked into the pits of his eyes. His pupils were as dark as his shoe-polish black hair, and they were ringed by an unusual reddish-gold color. Our eyes met for only a second, and mine went back down to the bar.

In that instant, I had seen plenty. Pain. Anger. And unless I'm a bad judge of character, which I'm not, a touch of crazy as well.

"Odd place to do business," I said, with practiced careless-ness.

"I'm looking for somebody." His voice was grave-dirt.

"Ain't we all?"

I saw movement out of the corner of my eye, and suddenly his hand was on the bar, palm-down. The back of his hand was a roadmap of blue veins, lined with tiny creases, and wiry black hairs stuck out in all directions. But what really caught my eye was the fifty-dollar bill underneath.

"Bartenders see things, know things," he muttered under his breath.

It was an occupational hazard, all right. I saw lots of things and knew things I wouldn't tell for twenty times that amount. But a fifty didn't walk in every day, and a G-note never did. I nodded my head slightly, to let him know I understood.

His hand suddenly balled into a fist, his veins becoming swollen with rage.

I smelled something. Smoke. I ran out to rescue the pot roast and was just sliding its black carcass out of the oven when my wife and daughter walked in.

"Order out for pizza?" I asked in greeting.

We ate the pizza, then I plowed ahead with the story. After a couple of pages, I was fighting for words, torturing myself through painful paragraphs, dangling from the cliff-edge of plot resolution like a sixth-grader's participle. What do I do with these people? I needed some fresh ideas.

After work the next day, I stopped down at Rocco's Place. Rocco was a short, paunchy Italian who was born into bartending. He wasn't a close friend, but I figured he was fair game as a model for my story. Marco. Rocco. Close, but he'd never know the difference. He probably dangled from the cliff-edge of literacy by a thin rope anyway.

His bar was much cleaner than the one in the story, but this place was too sterile to make good fiction. Readers wanted fantasy, not reality. They got plenty of reality. They got plenty of hard-backed chairs and plastic potted plants, scores of vapid muzak melodies piped through polyester speaker grills. I sat in one of the hard-backed chairs and ordered a beer.

"You that writer fella?" Rocco set a frothy brew in front of my face.

I was surprised. I didn't make a habit of telling people I was a "writer." I didn't wear tweed jackets with leather elbow patches or chew thoughtfully on a thick maple pipe. I might be crazy for trying to write, but I wasn't insane enough to advertise. But it was also nice to have my humble accomplishments recognized.

"I've published a little," I said, trying not to swell.

He wasn't looking at me anyway. He was wiping down the bar that was already so shiny customers were afraid to set down their drinks.

"Fella was in looking for you."

I stopped in mid-hoist, sloshing a little sticky liquid on my cuff. Who would look for me in a bar? I wasn't Hemingway. I could barely afford this beer, much less becoming one of Rocco's house fixtures.

"Big guy. Kinda mean-lookin'."

I laughed. "Let me guess. He thinks I'm messing with his wife, right?"

"Some people don't think it's funny. Especially certain husbands." His words were clipped and he kept his eyes down. "You're an okay guy. Don't spend a fortune, but ya never cause trouble. Been known to tip."

I was wondering if he was waiting for me to grease his palm, perhaps with my measly pocket change. But he continued.

"I know it's none of my business. But I thought I'd give you some advice, friend to friend. Keep an eye out for him. He's the dangerous type. Seen 'em before." He nodded to the perfect round bullethole that was the only blemish in the clean silver glass of the bar mirror.

I played along. "What did he look like?"

"Beefy guy, black hair, black like licorice kinda. Weird eyes, a color you hardly ever see. And he was wearing a big yella raincoat, and we ain't had rain for a week."

Karen must have put him up to this. She must have read my work-in-progress and planned this little joke. Surely she didn't think it was *me* that was having the affair?

I paid Rocco and left him to wipe up the ring my half-empty mug had made. I ran the three blocks home and went into the study to re-read what I had written last night. Sweat was pooling under my arms and my scalp was tingling, the way they always did when I was lost in an unfolding plot, only this time my intestines were unfolding along with it. The story carried me back into Marco's bar.

His hand suddenly balled into a fist, his veins becoming swollen with rage. I was staring at that fist, that big hunk of ham that looked like it could smash a city bus. I waited for it to relax, for the little muscles to stop twitching. When it was back in his pocket, leaving the bill, he said, "Wimpy little smart-assed writer type. Shifty-eyed know-it-all, been in here with a tall blonde. You woulda noticed her. Green eyes. Legs all the way down to the floor."

I had noticed, all right. Some hoity-toity wiseacre getting a looker like that, and us lonely bartenders paying through the nose for our company.

"What of 'em?" I asked.

"The fifty's for you. A fringe benefit of knowing things. And it's got a twin here in my pocket."

"Knowin' is cheap, but sayin' ain't."

Out of the corner of my eye, I saw a greasy smile slip across his face.

"Double or nothing, then. The double's for forgetting you ever saw me."

"Saw who?"

He laid another three fifties down on the bar. I eyed the joint in the mirror to make sure no one was watching. Then I swept the money away with my towel and had it in my pocket, where it would stay until I caught up with Leanna tonight.

"Lives three blocks down. Number 216 East."

He stood up, making an awfully big shadow on the scum-stained bar. Then the shadow, and the man in the yellow slicker, were gone. I felt sorry for that weeny little guy. Any minute now, he was gonna hear a knocking on his door—

The words danced in golden orange on the black screen of the word processor. Bad writing. A little too much Spillane and Chandler. The story had gotten away. Time to dive in, chop out its heart. Where to begin? Better finish reading it first.

A pounding on the door interrupted my thoughts.

—knocking on his door, then he's going to hear a yell, a crazy voice of phlegm and bitterness-

The crazy voice that was outside the apartment door, yelling "Hey, scumbag, open up or I'll bust the door down"; yelling "I'll make you pay for all the misery you caused"; yelling "Nobody's going to mess around with my wife, especially some snot-nosed fancy boy like you."

—kicking at the door with those big heavy boots, reaching inside that canary yellow slicker, grabbing a fistful of cold gat—

- 141 -

And the boots were on my door, making the hinges groan under the splintery strain.

—busting through and standing over the poor little loser, who's lookin' up at his killer, beggin', pleadin', offerin' up money he ain't got and prayin' to a God he don't believe in—

And the man in the yellow slicker is standing at the study door, holding a gun, his reddish-gold eyes blazing with insane hatred. I can see his finger tightening on the trigger. It's like a Stephen King story gone south, without the plot twists. Writer's character becomes real and comes to get him. It's been done too many times. Too trite even for me.

But the smell of metal and tension is too real, and the door is hanging like a wino from a boxcar.

—and he's sittin' at his little writing desk with his wimpy finger over the "delete" button, all he's got to do is press it and the man will go away. But he can't bring himself to do it. His work is too precious, too IMPORTANT to wipe out.

I take two hot slugs to the head, feel my brains begin their awkward eternal journey to the study wall. In its last moment of awareness, the ruined cerebellum searches frantically for a tidy ending, some way to bring the plot to completion, only it's much too far gone, much too hopeless, and the curtain of darkness...no, the veil of shadows...no, the wall of nothingness descends...

When Sil came home from work, he found Karen sitting in the study, staring at the word processor. The screen was full, and her face was orange in its glow. "What are you doing in here?" he asked.

"Oh, just messing around."

"Working on something?"

"I figured since everybody else was playing 'writer,' I might as well try my hand at it. Put myself in your shoes, to coin another cliché. Walk a mile in your gloves. But it's a lot harder than I thought. I believe I'd better take Faulkner's advice and kill my darlings."

She was reaching out to press the "delete" button when Sil caught her wrist. "Don't I get to read it first?"

"Well, if you really want to. But promise not to make fun of me."

"After some of the garbage I've written?"

Karen got up and let Sil take the chair. She said, "At least one good thing came out of this. Now I understand how you get so caught up in this stuff. You writers are nuts."

"That's *we* writers, dear." Sil laughed. He loved her. He began reading.

I was wiping down the bar with an old shirt rag when he came in. The man in the yellow slicker. I saw him without looking up...

Metabolism

The city had eyes.

It watched Elise from the glass squares set into its walls, walls that were sheer cliff faces of mortar and brick. She held her breath, waiting for them to blink. No, not eyes, only *windows*. She kept walking.

And the street was not a tongue, a long black ribbon of asphalt flesh that would roll her into the city's hot jaws at any second. The parking meter poles were not needly teeth, eager to gnash. The city would not swallow her, here in front of everybody. The city kept its secrets.

And the people on the sidewalk— how much did they know? Were they enemy agents or blissful cattle? The man in the charcoal-gray London Fog trenchcoat, the *Times* tucked under his elbow, dark head down and hands in pockets. A gesture of submission or a crafted stance of neutrality?

The blue-haired lady in the chinchilla wrap, her turquoise eyeliner making her look like a psychedelic raccoon. Was the lady colorblind or had she adopted a clever disguise? And were her mincing high-heeled steps carrying her to a midlevel townhouse or was she on some municipal mission?

That round-faced cabdriver, his black mustache brushing the bleached peg of his cigarette, the tires of his battered yellow cab nudged against the curb. Were his eyes scanning the passersby in hopes of a fare, or was he scouting for plump prey?

Elise tugged on her belt, wrapping her coat more tightly around her waist. The thinner one looked the better. Not that she had to rely on illusion. Her appetite had been buried with the other things of her old blind life, ordinary pleasures like window shopping and jogging. She had once traveled these streets voluntarily.

Best not to think of the past. Best to pack the pieces of it away like old toys in a closet. Perhaps someday she could open that door, shed some light, blow off the dust, oil the squeaky parts, and resume living. But for now, living must be traded for surviving.

She sucked in her cheeks, hoping she looked as gaunt as she felt. The wisp of breeze that blew up the street, more carbon monoxide than oxygen, was not even strong enough to ruffle the fringe on the awning above that shoeshop. But she felt as if the breeze might sweep her across the broken concrete, sending her tumbling and skittering like a cellophane candy wrapper. Sweeping her toward the city's throat.

She dared a glance up at the twenty-story tower of glass to her right. Eyes, eyes, eyes. Show no fear. Stare the monster in the face. It thinks itself invisible.

What a perfectly blatant masquerade. The city was rising from the earth, steel beams and guywire and cinderblock assembling right before their human eyes. Growing bold and hard and reaching for the sky, always bigger, bigger. How could everyone be so easily fooled?

Forget it, Elise. Maybe it reads minds. And you don't want to let it know what you're up to. You can keep a secret as well as it can.

She turned her gaze down to the tips of her shoes. There, just like a good city dweller is supposed to do. Count the cracks. Blend in. Be small.

Ignore the windowfront of the adult bookstore you pass. Don't see the leather whips, the rude plastic rods that gleam like eager rockets, the burlesque mockery of human flesh displayed on the placards. And the next window, plywooded and barred like an abandoned prison, "Liquor" hand-painted in dull green letters across the dented steel door beside it.

All to keep us drugged, dazed with easy pleasure. Elise knew. If it let us have our little amusements, then we wouldn't flee. We'd stay and graze on lust and drunkenness, growing fat and sleepy and tired and dull.

She flicked her eyes to the sky overhead, ignoring the sharp spears of the building-tops, with their antennae for ears. The low red haze meant that night was falling. The city constantly exhaled smog, so thick now that the sun barely peeped down onto the atrocities that were committed under its yellow eye. Even from the vigilant universe, the city kept its secrets.

Elise felt only dimly aware of the traffic that clogged the streets. Not streets. The arteries of the city. The cars rattled past, with raspy breath and an occasional growl of impatience. In the distance, somewhere on the far side of the city, sirens wailed. Sirens, or the screams of victims, face-to-face with the horrible thing that had crouched around them for years, cold and stone-silent one moment but alive and hungry the next.

Can't waste pity on them. The unwritten code of city life. Inbred indifference. Ignorance is bliss. A natural social instinct developed from decades of being piled atop one another like coldcuts in a grocer's counter. Or was the code taught, learned by rote, instilled upon them by a stern master who had its own best interests at heart?

And what would its heart be like? The sewers, raw black sludge snaking through its veins? The hot coal furnaces that huffed away in basements, leaking steam from corroded pipes? Or the electrical plant, a Gorgon's wig of wire sprouting from its roof, sending its veins into the apartments and office towers and factories so that no part of the city was untouched?

Or was it, as she suspected, heartless? Just a giant meat-eating cement slab of instinct?

She had walked ten blocks now. Not hurriedly, but steadily and with purpose. Perhaps like a thirty-year-old woman out for a leisurely stroll, headed to the park to watch from a bench while the sun set smugly over the jagged skyline. Maybe out to the theater, for an early seat at a second-rate staging of *Waiting For Godot*. Not like someone who was trying to escape.

No. Don't think about it.

She hadn't meant to, but now that the thought had risen from the murky swamp of subconsciousness, she turned it over in her mind, mentally fingering it like a mechanic checking out a carburetor.

No one escaped. At least no one she knew. They all slid, bloody and soft and bawling, from their mother's wombs into the arms of the city. Fed on love and hopes and dreams. Fed on lies.

She had considered taking a cab, hunching down in the back seat until the city became only a speck in the rear-view mirror. But she had seen the faces of the cabbies. They were too robust, too thick-jowled. Such as they should have been taken long ago. No, they were in on it.

And she had shuddered at the thought of stepping onto a city bus, hearing the hissing of the airbrakes and the door closing behind her like a squealing mouth. Delivering her not to the outskirts, but to the belly of the beast. They were *city* buses, after all.

Walking was the only way. So she walked. And the night fell around her, in broken scraps at first, furry shadows and gray insubstantial wedges. Lights came on in the buildings around her, soft pale globes and amber specks and opalescent blue stars and yellow-green windowsquares. Pretty baubles to pacify the masses.

She felt the walls slide toward her, closing in on her under the cloak of darkness. Don't panic, she told herself. Eyes straight ahead. You don't need to look to know the scenery. Sheer concrete, double-doors drooling with glass and rubber, geometrical orifices secreting the noxious effluence of consumption.

She thought perhaps she was safe. She was thin. But her sister Leanna had been thin. So thin she had been desired as a model, wearing long sleek gowns and leaning into the greedy eye of the camera, or preening in bathing suits on mockup beaches in highrise studios. So wonderfully waifish that she had graced the covers of the magazines that lined the checkout racks. Such a fine sliver of flesh that she had been lured to Los Angeles on the promise of acting work.

They said that she'd hopped on a plane to sunny California, was lounging around swimming pools and getting to know all the right people. Elise had received letters in which Leanna told about the palm trees and open skies, about mountains and moonlit bays. About the bit part she'd gotten in a movie, not much but a start.

Elise had gone to see the movie. She sat in a shabby,

gum-tarred seat, the soles of her shoes sticking to the sloping cement floor. There she'd seen Leanna, up on the big screen, walking and talking and doing all the things that she used to do back when she was alive. Leanna, pale and ravishing and now forever young and two-dimensional.

Oh, but putting her in a film could be easily faked, just like the letters. A city that could control and herd a million people would go to such lengths to keep its secrets. All she knew was that Leanna was gone, gobbled up by some man-hole or doorway or the hydraulic jaws of a sanitation truck.

And she knew others who had gone missing. Out to the country, they said. Away on vacation. Business trips. Weddings and funerals to attend. But never heard from again. Some of them overweight, some healthy, some muscular, some withered.

So being thin was no guarantee. But she suspected that it helped her chances. If only she was light enough that the sidewalk didn't measure her footsteps.

She'd reached unfamiliar territory now. A strange part of the city. But wasn't it all strange? Alien caves, too precise to be man-made? Elevators, metal boxes dangling at the ends of rusty spiderwebs? Storm grates grinning and leering from street corners? Lampposts bending like alloyed preying mantises?

The faces of the few pedestrians out at that hour were clouded with shadows. Did the white arrowtips of their eyes flick ever so slightly at her as she passed? Did they sense a traitor in their midst? Were they glaring jealously at her tiny bones, the skin stretched taut around her skull, her meatless appearance?

The smell of donuts wafted across her face, followed by the bittersweet tang of coffee. Her nostrils flared in arousal in spite of herself. She looked into the window of the deli. Couples were huddled at round oak tables, the steam of their drinks rising in front of them like smoke from chemical fires. They were chatting, laughing, eating from loaded plates, reading magazines, acting as if they had all the time in the world. They had tasted the lie, and found it palatable.

She tore her eyes away. They traded pleasure for inevitability. Dinner would one day be served, and they would find themselves on the plate, pale legs splayed indignantly upward, wire mesh at their heads for garnish. Well, she had no tears to spare for them. One chose one's own path.

Her path had started about a year ago, shortly before Leanna left. Not left, was *taken*, she reminded herself. Elise's understanding had started with the television set. The TV stood on a Formica cabinet against the sheetrock wall of her tiny apartment, flashing colorful images at her. Showing her all the things she was being offered. Brand new sedans. Dental floss and mouthwash. The other white meat. The quicker-picker-upper. The uncola.

The television made things attractive. The angle of the lighting, eye-pleasing color schemes, seductive layouts and product designs. Straight teeth cutting white lines across handsome tan faces. And behind those rigid smiles, she had seen the fear. Fear masquerading as vacuousness. Threatened puppets spouting monologues, the sales pitch of complacency.

She had found other clues. The police, for instance. Never around when one needed them. Delivery vans with unmarked sideboards, prowling at all hours. Limousines, long and dark-glassed advertisements for conspicuous consumption. Around-the-clock convenience stores and neon billboards. A quiet conspiracy in the streets, unobserved among the bustle and noise of daily life, everyone too busy grabbing merchandise to stop and smell the slagheap acid of the roses.

But Elise had noticed. Saw how the city grew, stretching obscenely higher, ever thicker and more oppressive and powerful. And she had made the connection. The city fed itself. It was getting bloated on the human hors d'oevres that tracked across its tongue like live chocolate-covered ants.

When one knew where to look, one saw signs of its life. The pillars of filthy smoke that marked its exhalations, the iridescent ribbons of its urine that trickled through the gutters, the sweat of the city clinging to moist masonry. The gray snowy ash of its dandruff, the chipped gravel of its sloughed dead skin. The crush of the walls, squeezing in like cobbled teeth, outflanking and surrounding its prey. And all the while spinning its serenade of sonic booms and fire alarms, automobile horns and fastfood speakers, ringing cash registers and clattering jackhammers.

Elise had bided her time, staying cautious, not telling a soul. Whom could she trust? Her neighbors might have an ear pressed to the wall. The city employed thousands.

So she had hid behind her closed door, the TV turned to face the corner. Oh, she had still gone to work, leaving every weekday morning for her post at the bank. It was important to keep up appearances. But, once home, she locked herself in and pulled the windowshade. She turned on the radio, just in case the city was using its ears, but she always tuned to commercial-free classical stations. Music to eat sweets by.

Her workmates had expressed concern.

"You're nothing but skin and bones. You feeling okay?"

"You're getting split-ends, girl."

"You look a little pale. Maybe you should go to the doctor, Elise."

As if she were going to listen to them, with their new forty-dollar hairstyles every week and retirement accounts and lawyer husbands and City Council wives and panty hose and wristwatches and power ties and deodorant. Elise only smiled and shook her head and pretended. Took care of the customers and kept her accounts balanced.

And she had plotted. Steeled herself. Got up her nerve and slung her handbag over her shoulder and walked out of the bank after work and headed downtown. She kept reminding herself that she had nothing to lose.

And now she was almost free. She could taste the cleaner air, could feel the pressure of the hovering structures ease as she drew nearer to the outskirts. But now darkness descended, and she wasn't sure if that brought the city to keen-edged life or sent it fat and dull into dreamy slumber.

She passed the maw of a subway station. A few people jogged down the steps into the bright throat of the tunnel. She thought of human meat packed into the smooth silver tubes and shot through the intestines of the city.

She walked faster now, gaining confidence and strength as hope spasmed in her chest like a pigeon with a broken wing. She could see the level horizon, a beautiful black flatness only blocks ahead. Buildings skulked here and there, but they were short and squat and clumsy.

The road was devoid of traffic, the dead-end arms of the city. The streetlights thinned, casting weak cones of light every few hundred feet.

Her footsteps echoed down the empty street, bouncing into the dark canyons of the side alleys. The hollowness of the sound enhanced her sense of isolation. She felt exposed and vulnerable. Easy meat.

Her ears pricked up, tingling.

A noise behind her, out of step with her echo.

Breathing.

The spiteful puff of a forklift, its tines aimed for her back? A fire hydrant, hissing in anger at her audacity? The sputtering gasp of a sinuous power cable?

Footsteps.

A rain of lightbulbs, dropping in her wake? The concrete slabs of the sidewalk, folding upon themselves like an accordion, chasing her heels? A street sign hopping after her like a crazed pogo stick?

Not now. Not when she was so close.

But did she really expect that the city would let her simply step out of its garden?

She ducked into an alley, even though the walls gathered on three sides. Instinct had driven her into the darkness. But then, why shouldn't the city control her instinct? It owned everything else.

And now it moved in for the kill, taking its due. Now she was ripe fruit to be plucked from the chaotic fields the city had sown, a harvest to be reaped by rubber belts and pulleys and metal fins.

Elise stumbled into a garbage heap, knocking over a trash can in her blindness. She fell face-first into greasy cloth and rotten paper and moldering food scraps. She felt a sting at her knee as she rolled into broken glass.

She turned on her back, resigned to her fate. She would die quietly, but she wanted to see its face. Not the face it showed to human eyes, the one of glass panes and cornerstones and sheet metal. She wanted to see its true face.

She saw a silhouette, a blacker shape against the night. A splinter of silver catching a stray strand of distant streetlight, flashing at her like a false grin. A featureless machine pressing close, its breath like stale gin and cigarette butts and warm copper.

Its voice fell from out of the thick air, not with the jarring clang of a bulldozer or the sharp rumble of tractor trailer rig, but as a harsh whisper.

"Gimme your money."

So the city had sent this puny agent after her? With all its great and awesome might, its monumental obelisks, its omnipotent industry, its cast-iron claws, its impregnable asphalt hide, its pressurized fangs, it sends *this*?

The city had a sense of humor. How wonderful!

She thought of that old children's story, the "Three Billy Goats Gruff," how the smaller ones had offered up the larger ones to slake the evil troll's appetite. She laughed, filling the cramped alley with her cackles. "A skinny thing like me would hardly be a mouthful for you," she said, the words squeezing out between giggles.

She felt the city's knife press against her chest, heard a quick snip, and felt her handbag being lifted from her shoulder. The straps hung like dark spaghetti, and the city tucked the purse against its belly. The city, small and dark andhuman.

Now she saw it. The human machine had a face the color of bleached rags, dingy mopstrings dangling down over the hot sparks of eyes. Thin wires sprouted above the coin-slot mouth. Why, he was *young*. The city eats its young.

"You freakin' city folks is all nuts," the city said, then ran into the street, back under the safe sane lights.

Its words hung over Elise's head, but they'd come from another world. A world of platinum and fiberglass, locomotives and razor blades. The real world. Not her world.

As the real city awoke and busied itself with its commerce and caffeine, it might have seen Elise sprawled among the rubble of a rundown neighborhood, flanked by empty wine bottles and used condoms and milk cartons graced with the photographs of anonymous children. It might have smelled her civet perfume, faint but there, which she had dabbed on her neck in an attempt to smell like everyone else. It might have heard the wind fluttering the collar of her Christian Dior blouse, bought so that she could blend in with the crowd. It might have felt the too-light weight of her frail body, wasted by a steady diet of fear. It might have tasted the human salt where tears of relief had dried on her cheeks.

It might have divined her dreams, intruded on her sleep to find goats at the wheels of steamrollers, corrugated snakes slithering as endlessly as escalators among gelatin hills, caravans of television antennas dancing across flat desert sands, and a flotilla of cellular phones on a windswept ocean of antifreeze, an owl and a pussycat in each.

If the city sensed these things, it remained silent.

The city kept its secrets.

The Boy Who Saw Fire

He dreamed of hot things.

Red peppers curled like the tips of elveshoes. Stove eyes, their orange coils glaring menacingly. Asphalt, soft and black and casting ribbons of heat on a summer day. Steambaths, mists of boiling dews. And, at the center of his dreams, the point around which these fiery molten ores revolved, was the golden hell of the sun.

He dreamed of cities on fire, of office-workers stumbling from doorways like animated matchsticks, their hair aflame. Of yellow cabs driving down buckling streets, smoke churning from open windows; of sidewalks writhing like ant-covered snakes. Of glass melting in towering buildings, the warm spun taffy of slag running forty floors down. Of satellite dishes withering like sunflowers in a drought. Of hot gases pluming from broken water mains. Of pedestrians swelling and dripping grease like plump wieners on a Fourth of July grill.

He dreamed of a blanket of black oily smog covering the ground, the sky filled with a billion particles of soot, pillars and mushrooms of gray clouds dancing in celebration, twisting like twinkle-toed tornadoes among the hot coals, dead fogs battling the firelight for shadowy dominance, blistering winds urging the flames to wicked heights.

And as the embers died, as the immolating pyres consumed themselves, as the land lay charred and crisp and barren, he dreamed of spring rains, gentle drizzles that carried off the ash in quiet rivulets, waterdrops that dissipated and dissolved the thick smoke, the dark charcoal ruins swept away by the dustbroom wind. In his dreams, a new sun hovered, a cool and gentle gift-giver, a bringer of change, a rose-colored harbinger.

This morning, as always, he awoke in a sweat, as if the fires and rains had been at work on the plain of his forehead. The real sun was stabbing through his bedroom window with an accusing eye, reprimanding him for sleeping late. He kicked off the blankets and stood up and stretched, his belly-button yawning between pajama halves. He knelt over and tugged up his socks, which had been flagging out beyond his stubby toes.

"Billy, breakfast is ready," his mom called from downstairs. He rubbed his eyes.

"Be down in a sec," he yelled back, then changed into his blue jeans and T-shirt. The sky outside his window was blue and cloudbare. It looked like it was going to be another scary summer day. He jogged downstairs.

His mom kissed him on the top of his head. "Playing ball today?"

"Some of the guys talked about it yesterday." Billy didn't mention they they hadn't invited him. He sat at the table and looked at his plate. Two strips of bacon, a circular sausage patty, and two eggs. Sunny side up. The eggs were like yellow eyes.

"I don't think I'm hungry this morning, Mom."

"Are you feeling okay, honey?" She pressed her wrist against his forehead. "I hope you're not getting another one of those fevers."

"I'm fine."

"You feel a little warm to me."

That's because I dream of fire, he thought. And when I wake up, the fire is hiding behind everything like red shadows. It's there in the big oak tree out in the yard. The top where the leaves catch the sunlight is trying to be a torch.

See that fire hydrant by the sidewalk, just outside the white picket fence? If firemen came by and turned the big plug with their wrenches, lava would spew out and burn the grass. And the driveway is a vein of coal, waiting to be lit so it can smolder forever.

"It's probably just because of July," Billy said.

"Hmm. Well, you better take it easy today. Maybe you should stay inside in the air-conditioning."

"Aw, can't I go down and play by the creek?"

"I told you to stay away from that nasty water. I don't care if it *is* shady down there under the trees."

"But, Mom—"

"No 'buts' about it, young man. Or you can get your pajamas back on and get right back in bed."

In bed, where the heat came to him from somewhere inside his head or heart. But he knew he couldn't argue with Mom.

He poked at the egg yolks until they bled ochre. He forked off a small piece and put it in his mouth. He swallowed, hoping he wouldn't get burned. After the egg slid down his throat, he smiled at his mom. "I'm getting a little appetite now."

"You've got to keep your strength up. An eleven-year-old needs good nutrition."

She crossed the kitchen, her high heels clacking on the floor tiles, and went to the bathroom, probably to check on her make-up before going off to work. Billy put his hand on his glass of orange juice, then drew back as if he had received an electric shock. The liquid was so— so very *orange*.

He much preferred milk, the cool white silky smooth

- 159 -

drink. White reminded him of the hospital, where he had spent most of the spring, back when the winter breezes had flickered and died and the last snow had melted away. The days had started getting longer and the sun glared like a baleful enemy. And the fevers had come.

An endless round of doctors poked and prodded him, put the cold metal discs on chest. But the fevers went away when he was tucked in the windowless room where the only light came from the weak fluorescent tubes. The greenish light made everybody look sick, even the nurses in their sterile uniforms and flat hair.

After a week, after the needle-marks in his arms were like red constellations from the blood tests, the doctors had shrugged their shoulders and scratched their beards and adjusted their eyeglasses. They sent him home, telling his parents that he needed rest and a good diet, and to let them know if the symptoms recurred. His father held his hand as they walked out the hospital's glass doors.

His father's hand felt like a volcanic mitten. Billy's palm began sweating. And the sun was out that day, high and bright and harmful. He had raised his forearm against the light, trying to shield his eyes.

"You'll get used to it," Dad said, smiling down with wide lips. Sometimes Billy saw red specks in his father's pupils, as if ethereal fires were burning inside. But that day, Dad had been wearing sunglasses, and Billy saw only his own pale face staring back.

"You're looking a little better, honey," Mom said, but Billy saw the lie sitting on her tongue between the even rows of her teeth.

"He'll live. We always have," Dad said.

They brought him home and took him to his bedroom and laid him under the cool sheets. And he sweated away April and May, surrounded by those blue walls. His mother brought his meals on a vinyl tray. His father worked nights and slept most of the day, but always came up to read Billy bedtime stories before leaving for his job. His father would close the book just before the sun dipped below the horizon and the beautiful velvet curtain of night fell over the earth outside the window.

His father would wish him goodnight, wipe his brow, and kiss Billy's forehead, then close the door and leave Billy to his thoughts. And Billy would twist the sheets, curl the pillow against his belly, and fight the heaviness in his lids. He would stare at the ceiling he couldn't see and count the dolphins leaping out of glittering bays, or imagine a waterfall pouring down the walls and battering him with silver-blue drops.

But sleep always won, and the conflagrations roared across his dreams. He was afraid to tell his parents about the dreams. He didn't want to disappoint them. And his mother wouldn't let him play outside if he complained. So the night-fires raged on and Billy suffered in silence and awoke each day with pajamas that were damp with perspiration.

Billy pretended that he was fine, and talked about going to school in the fall. Now he was eating downstairs and sometimes his mother would let him watch television. She was working again and felt that Billy was well enough to stay home with his sleeping father. Billy kept busy all day drinking large tumblers of ice water, wiping the cool dew from the glass against his face and sucking on the ice cubes. But now he had *orange* juice, and it looked like heat to him.

He picked up his napkin and wrapped it around the glass, ran to the sink and poured the offending liquid down the drain. Then he snuck back to the table, his socks sliding on the floor. He was just settling back in his chair when his mother returned.

"You've got a big-boy thirst today," she said, fussing with an earring. The tiny ruby in it caught some light coming through the kitchen window and glowed fervidly. Billy winced against the pain and looked across the room until his eyes came to rest on a shadowy corner. When he turned back to his mother, the fire was out and she was walking towards the door.

"I'll be back at noon. Get yourself to bed, now," she called over her shoulder. Billy went up the stairs and listened until he heard his mom's car head down the street. Then he went to his closet and got out his bike helmet with its blue-green visor. He pushed his feet into his sneakers and slid on a pair of black biking gloves. He went downstairs, through the kitchen, and into the adjoining garage.

His Huffy ten-speed was leaning against the wall beneath the tool rack that held Dad's shovel, rake, and hedge trimmers. He rolled the Huffy to the end of the garage and pressed the button that raised the door, hoping the noise wouldn't wake his father. Sunlight poured in like scalding water. He staggered against the light, then regained his balance and mounted the bike, and in a moment he was down the driveway, pumping his legs and hunching over the curved handlebars.

As he turned onto the street and gained speed, the rushing wind cooled his body. The sunlight chased him, but he was moving so swiftly that the beams scarcely had time to settle on his skin. He turned south at the corner and was shaded by a row of old oaks that lined the sidewalks like sentries. He stopped at the next intersection, straddling the bike on his tiptoes as he braced himself for the worst part of his trip.

Before him was a sun-splashed strip of highway, open and cruel and carless, with not a phone-pole's worth of shade. The heat would rip through his body in needles and nails of fiery pain. Even the visor wouldn't fully soften the glare that would prick his eyes. He was sweating now, but it was the sweat of exertion, not the sweat of fevers and dreams.

On the other side of the street, the woods beckoned. Honeysuckle vines laced through the scrub locust and kudzu had gained a healthy foothold in the end that bordered the weedy lot of an unsold house. The crooked branches of the pines stretched out and interlaced to form a canopy. The only beauty of the place was in its daylight dark, the wonderful unbroken shadow that stretched under the foliage.

Billy took a deep breath and leaned his weight forward and he was off in a flash. The sun shot ions and light-arrows at him, but most were off the mark. He dodged and weaved, then he was across the swollen river of sunshine, his front tire bumping up at the curb, and he was embraced by the shade of the woods. His feet made no noise on the carpet of pine needles and he could hear a finch chattering somewhere above him. Then he was at the creek and he kneeled down and put his face near the cold water.

A round concrete pipe stuck out of the slope, spilling water from its black mouth. The water gurgled into a pool, splattering off round stones and sending drops of spray arcing into the air. Billy let some of the drops roll down his face like joyful tears. He lay on his stomach and looked into the pool. Water spiders skittered across its surface, leaving pockmarks of tracks that faded in an eyeblink. The damp smell of muddy black leaves and moss filled his nostrils. He was safe. Here, no fire could burn.

Billy rolled onto his back and looked up through the trees. He could see patches of blue sky in the cracks, calm and cloudless. The sun would be up there somewhere, boiling in anger at his escape. He closed his eyes and put sun and fire and red and orange out of his mind. Before he knew it, he was asleep.

Billy dreamed that he was undersea. Somehow, he knew that he had drowned. He tried his limbs and found they still worked, though a bit awkwardly. The world moved in slow motion, graceful fish finning silently past his ears and sinuous eels winding across the sandy bottom. He looked up from the deep blue belly of death and saw the light high above. He was about to push off and make for it when he remembered the evil sun. Then he was struggling to keep himself from floating, fighting the peaceful drift of nothingness.

He awoke with his back in the dirt and leaves. He looked out at the houses that surrounded the woods and saw by their long shadows that it was afternoon. Mom would be home soon. He ran up the bank to his ten-speed and wheeled it to the street, winced against the daylight, then raced the sun back to the house.

As he entered the kitchen through the garage, his dad's voice called to him. "Hi, Billy. Where have you been?"

The words seemed to have come from the air, or out of the heating vents, or maybe down the chimney. There was no accusation in them, only curiosity. Billy whirled and saw his dad sitting in a dark corner of the living room.

"Uh— I went for a bike ride."

"Out in the sun?"

"Yeah. Mom said it was okay, and that it would probably do me some good to get some fresh air."

Billy could see his dad's eyes glimmering in the darkness, two bright but cool moons. He stepped into the living room toward his dad, his sneakers seeming to float on the carpet, he walked so softly. Dad rarely yelled at him, but he was afraid he'd be in trouble if his dad caught him in a lie.

"Looks like a beautiful day outside." Dad said it as a query, a gambit. Did he know?

"Yeah, but it's almost too hot."

"Makes a guy want to find a cool place and hide from the sun."

Billy nodded. He could make out the edge of his dad's body now, a darker silhouette among the shadows.

"How are you feeling? Any fever?" Dad's voice was smoky and deep.

"I feel good. I think I'm getting better now."

"It's okay if you're not. You can't rush things. Just take it easy."

"Sure, Dad." Billy really *did* feel better. His secret was still safe.

Dad stood up, and it was as if the shadows fluttered around him, falling from his shoulders in black rags. He walked over to Billy and put his warm hand on his son's head. Billy was struck by a vivid image of the burning cities of his dreams, then they, too, flickered away, like woodsmoke carried off by the wind.

"I'm going back to bed now. Just knock on the door if you need anything," his dad said. Billy watched the way Dad avoided the sunlight while walking across the living room, staying in the black island cast by the shadow of the couch, then lingering under the lampshade before entering the kitchen. Billy heard a soft squeaking on the stairs and a door closing.

"We'll survive. We always have," Billy muttered to himself. What had his dad meant? He remembered back in the third grade when the class had to give speeches about what their parents did. Most of the children were the offspring of doctors, lawyers, accountants, and professors, the smattering of professionals that could afford to live in this upper-class district. One shamefaced girl admitted that her father was a fireman and her mother was a cocktail waitress. One boy's father was a pro baseball player, but he admitted that his father wasn't good enough yet to be on his own baseball card. It was as if he had confessed that his dad was a drug dealer, the way he shuffled back to his desk with his head hanging down.

When it was Billy's turn, he stood in front of the class and looked out at the sea of sniffling faces. He glanced out the window at the sun-splashed playground, where kids were jumping rope and kicking soccer balls. The light didn't seem to bother them, because they were laughing and running and no one seemed worried about the big hot enemy in the sky. Billy cleared his throat and spoke.

"My mom works at a bank, counting people's money," he said, then his voice fell away. "And my dad—"

He looked at the crazy patterns in the ceiling tiles, then back down at the gray floor. He didn't quite know how to put it into words. He had stayed awake nights, thinking about it. Nights when he knew the fire would come in dreams, red and vengeful.

"My dad puts out the sun."

The class was silent, dull as cows.

"He pushes it down in the sky and grabs the corners of night and pulls the darkness up over the world like a blanket."

Then the laughter started. It began as a birdish twitter somewhere in the back. Then a snicker burst out two aisles over. Next a guffaw, follow by a hoot. Then the whole class erupted, a choir of hilarity that disturbed classes up and down the hall. Even Miss McAllister had her hand over her mouth, trying to hide her smile.

Billy felt his face burn in embarrassment. His cheeks and ears tingled. He wanted to run, but his feet were as heavy as dictionaries. He closed his eyes tight, squeezing tears from their corners.

Miss McAllister tried to settle the class down. She stood in front of her desk with her hands on her hips. Then she turned and tapped a ruler on the back of a chair. Slowly the laughter faded, like boiling water reduced to a simmer, an occasional bubble rippling but the surface calm.

"That's some imagination you have, Billy," she said. She was still smiling, her pink lipstick glistening in the light. Billy looked at her and felt his eyes darken. He didn't know how he could feel such a thing, but he did. And he knew that if he looked in a mirror, there would be little specks of fire in his pupils, just like Dad's. He returned to his seat.

He put his head on his desk and imagined his classmates with their skin dripping from their bones like hot wax running down a candle. He pictured Miss McAllister sinking into the sun, screaming as the thermonuclear furnace reduced her to vapor. He daydreamed a rain of molten orange ingots falling from the sky, piercing holes in the roof of the schoolhouse and sizzling the children out on the playground. In his mind, the fire swept across the schoolyard like a yellow tide, turning laughter to screams. And behind the tide came the clouds, a dark blank nothingness that would suffocate the ashes. He rode the bus home in a sweat.

Even now, three years later, he still carried the memory of that day inside him, like a small ember kept alive in his chest. He had gained the reputation of being an oddball. The bullies had culled him from the herd like wolves culling a weak lamb from the flock. They called him the "Sundance Kid," and pushed him around while the girls stood by and laughed and dared each other to kiss him.

No one seemed surprised when he got sick. The fevers had plagued him off and on, and his attendance record was spotty. His mom rushed him to the doctor every few weeks until the condition landed him in the hospital. His dad was sympathetic to his suffering, but Billy thought he saw secrets lurking in his dad's eyes, as if they were hiding something that all the doctors in the world couldn't diagnose.

Billy went to the shadowed corner of the living room where his dad had been sitting. He felt better here, where the light didn't stab and the cool air swirled from the air conditioning vent. He clicked on the television with the remote, but the flickering screen hurt his eyes so he turned it off. Mom's car backed into the garage and she walked into the kitchen.

"Hi, guy. Feeling okay?"

"Sure, Mom. I stayed in like you told me to. Dad kept me company for a while."

- 167 -

"He was up today?"

"Just for a little bit." Billy wondered if his dad would tell her he'd been outside.

"Well, he needs his rest. He works hard."

"Mom, what does Dad <u>do</u>?"

She frowned. "You'll have to ask him. I can't really explain it."

That night, when his dad came to see Billy to bed, Billy said, "Remember when I was little and I asked what your job was, and you told me you tucked in the sun? And you said you'd explain when I was ready?"

His dad put a warm hand on his shoulder and smiled. "Of course. I remember everything I ever told you."

"Well, am I ready yet?"

His dad laughed, and Billy thought he saw smoke come out of his open mouth. "Well, I guess you're getting to be a big boy now. Nearly a man."

Billy puffed out his chest under the blankets.

"Well, like I told you when you were little, I tuck in the sun, just like I tuck you in. Didn't you ever wonder why we always put you to bed just before sunset?"

"But, Dad, they taught us all about gravity in science class, and how the earth spins and revolves around the sun, and that it's night when our side of the earth is turned away from the light."

"That's because they don't know about us."

"Us?"

"People have always looked for explanations for things they couldn't understand. A long time ago, people believed that the sun and the moon were gods, one ruling the day and one ruling the night. Then they thought the earth was the center of the universe, with the sun and the planets circling around it. Now they have the theories that they teach in school. Because it's better if people believe these things than to know the real truth."

"What is the truth?"

"Remember how you told what I did and the class laughed at you?"

Billy nodded, his belly inflamed at the memory.

"It's not good for them to know. It would make our work that much harder."

"What work? There's more to it than just the sun. I can tell by the way you're talking."

His dad sighed and looked out the window, then removed his sunglasses. The sun was setting like a bloody egg yolk, appearing to hover just over the horizon as if reluctant to yield control of the sky. He turned back to Billy with his lips tight. Billy saw yellow and orange flecks glittering in Dad's irises, and his face looked pained.

"I put the sun inside here." His dad pointed to his temple. Sweat was collecting on his brow and his teeth were clenched. He closed his eyes and grimaced as if he were swallowing a stone. Outside, the world was growing blue-gray as the last fingers of twilight clutched at the fabric of the day. Then the night rose like a black fog, cold and dead and soothing.

His dad's face paled, then the rosy color slowly returned. His irises were golden orange and his pupils were fiery crimson, the color of the heart of the sun. He smiled, like someone who had taken bitter medicine and knew the worst was over.

"Sunset is the hardest part," his dad said. "The sun doesn't like to be put to bed. If it had its way, it would shine non-stop."

Billy shuddered at the horror of the thought. He felt his dad trembling so hard that the mattress quivered.

"But I'm strong enough to keep it inside, so that the world can rest for a while. Then it gets too hot inside my head and I must let it out again. It's easier in the winter, when the wind is cold. But during summer, the sun is really hot and strong and angry, and I can't store it as long."

Billy tried to understand. Did this have anything to do with his dreams and night sweats?

"I give night to the world, just as my ancestors did before me. It has been our job since time began. We are the keepers of the oldest flame. Long ago, when there were many of us, ice covered most of the earth. But over the ages, as the sun grew older and stronger, our numbers dwindled. Now there's only us."

"Us?"

"You and me. And we must never surrender. Only we can douse the wrath of the sun, if only temporarily. Only we can give respite to a world that would otherwise be a cinder."

"But why *us*, Dad?"

"We are born to it, Billy. And someday, when I weaken and become parched and can no longer suppress the flames of the sun, then I will pass the torch to you, just as it was passed to me."

"You mean, Grandpa—?"

"You only saw him at night. Remember there at the end, just before he died? Everybody thought it was sickness. They were right, only not in the way they thought. He was burnt out, mentally baked away from decades of swallowing the fire."

Billy envisioned his grandpa, sweating beneath the sheets, the fever racing through his wasted body as the last days of his life ticked away in that nursing home. Even in his near-comatose state, Grandpa always knew when some nurse had opened the curtains and let the daylight stream through the window. How could the nurses know they were letting the conquerer in to revel over the bones of its vanquished foe? They had been taught that the sun was a healthy, life-giving thing, not a vile enemy.

"I've been fighting the sun a long time, Billy. Long enough to know its secrets and its tricks. And I will teach them to you when you're ready. Someday you will divide night from day. Someday you will rule the sun, at least for a few hours at a time."

"Is that why the sunshine hurts so much?"

"It knows its enemies."

"And my dreams—"

"Of the world on fire, in a blaze of yellow and orange glory? That's what happens when the solar power rages out of control. That's what we must prevent."

The world outside the window was black, a sheet of oblivion stretched tight across the sky and pegged in place by his dad's thoughts. Starlight was sprinkled across the tarry night.

"Why are there stars, Dad?" Billy asked. He rubbed his eyes. He was getting sleepy.

"There are no stars, only the sun breaking through in spots. We are imperfect."

"The moon?"

"The sun's idiot twin. It's harmless. Just the sun's way of reminding us that it's waiting for us to get tired."

Billy let his head drop back into the pillows. There was so much to figure out. "Does Mom know?"

"She suspects something, but she's only human. I've tried to spare her the worst of it. I only wish I could tell her why you have the fevers, so she wouldn't worry so much."

"When will the fevers stop?" Billy looked at his dad's sickly complexion. The skin had a bloodless pall, and a sheen of bright sweat glittered on his forehead.

Dad shook his head slowly from side to side. "It never ends. We burn until we burn up."

"But *why*?"

His dad shrugged. "Why is the earth flat? It is our nature to live just as it is the sun's nature to burn."

"What if we don't stop the sun?"

"Then the world burns instead of us."

Billy was quiet. He thought of the nice shady place in the woods, where he could press his cheek in the cool mud. So escape

- 171 -

would be only temporary, and long sweltering years lay ahead of him.

An idea came to him. He wondered if there was somebody who shepherded the wind, just as his dad controlled the sun. Someone whose cheeks were constantly sore from puffing and blowing.

And someone who made the rains fall and water flow, perhaps by crying, when the water only wanted to pool quietly.

And someone who held up the sky, who at this moment was telling his or her child about the evils that hovered above the clouds, waiting for a sliver of opening in which to descend. Might not there be all kinds of powers at work, each carefully and precariously balanced to make the world livable?

His dad must have sensed that he'd told Billy enough for one night. Dad was still strong, and even though he was probably sick of holding the stellar furnace in his head, he wasn't ready to surrender. He kissed Billy on the forehead, his scalding lips touching the equally warm skin of his son.

"Good night, Billy. I hope you dream of ice," he whispered. He turned out the light as he left.

Billy lay in the dark, contemplating the illusion of night. One day he would fight the sun. One day he would swallow fire. One day he would keep the world from becoming a funeral pyre, as he had seen it burning in his mind. As he had *wished* it to burn, back when he hated the world as much as he hated the sun. But tonight, it was enough to know the sun could be beaten.

He pressed his eyes closed, and his mind spun in bright circles until his thoughts disappeared into a perfect red and stormy sleep.

Constitution

On the third day, he felt the flesh loosening around his fingerbones.

He slipped into the bedroom and pulled on a pair of white silk gloves. Demora wouldn't notice, at least not right away. And he could always tell her that he was practicing a mime routine. She'd fall for that. She'd fall for anything, as long as the lie came from his lips.

"Randall, honey," Demora called from downstairs. She would be in the kitchen, pouring him a drink. Scotch with a half-pound of ice cubes. He could already picture the glass beaded with grotesque sweat.

He wished he himself could sweat. The summer heat had made his condition worse. The thunderstorm that afternoon had provided a brief respite. It rolled in at three just like clockwork. But time really had no meaning anymore, not since he had died. His wife called to him again.

"Yes, dear?" he answered, struggling to make his throat work smoothly. He touched his Adam's apple with one gloved hand.

"I've got a drinky-poo for you."

"I'll be right down."

He stopped at the bathroom on the way. He stood in front of the mirror and lifted his eyelids. No *tache noir* yet. Black eyes would be a dead giveaway.

He went into the living room. The drink rested on the coffee table. He gingerly settled into his easy chair. Demora had loaded his pipe so that it would be at his elbow, awaiting the touch of fire.

She came out of the kitchen, her gown disguising her huggable roundness. Her hair was up in a severe bun. It wasn't her best look. The bareness of her neck made her chins more noticeable. But she was still beautiful. She smiled.

"Hard day at work, dear?" Her voice was sparrow-light and cheerful.

"Not really."

Because he hadn't done anything. He went down to the theater and made sure he was visible, so that everyone would know that reliable old Randall was on the job. Then he sat in his office with the lights off, listening to the banging as the set designers prepped for "My Fair Lady." It was another world, out there between the curtains, a world that he could no longer have a part in. He would have cried if he could've summoned the necessary fluids.

"Dear?"

Demora's voice snapped him out of his reverie.

"Yes, my sweet?" he said, with a steady delivery. He had been a decent actor, once. He saw no reason why he couldn't pull off his greatest performance. The deceased Randall, starring as the living Randall, for a limited run only.

"Are you okay? You seem a little...I don't know."

Her eyes darkened with worry. It made her eyebrows vee on her forehead.

"I'm fine, dear. Right as rain, dandy as a doodle."

"Hmm. If you say so."

"I say so."

He lifted his drink. It was difficult. His strength was ebbing.

He sipped, then gulped. No taste. He wished he could feel the burn, the tingle, the glow, the cold, anything.

"Is it just right, my little honey-pot smooch?" Demora asked. She held one hand in front of her ample bosom, eager to please.

"Perfect," he said, forcing a smile. His lips were too dry. They felt as if they were about to split. He let the smile fade.

Randall fumbled for the pipe. All his little routines were now Herculean tasks. He stuck the pipe stem in his mouth and felt it against his wooden tongue. Demora pulled a lighter out of nowhere and thumbed a bright flame.

Heat. He sucked, lost for feeling, lost for pain, lost for comfort. He swallowed and didn't cough. Smoking was difficult now that he no longer breathed.

Demora hovered, flitting around his elbows like a rotund hummingbird, her speed belying her size. She unrolled the newspaper and draped it across his lap, then knelt to remove his shoes.

"No, darling," he said. She looked up, disappointed.

He was afraid that the stench would be overpowering.

"I may go for a walk later," he said.

She nodded and grinned.

It was only when she was handing him the television remote that she mentioned the gloves.

"Just a little change, my sweet," he said. He flexed his fingers. They felt like sausages encased in plastic sheaths.

The evening passed in the world outside. The sun made its weary trek down the sky. The crickets began their nightly complaining from the alleys. Streetlights hummed. Demora hummed, too. She was a mezzo-soprano.

They readied for bed. This was the worst time of all, the most awkward moment. Randall snuck to the bathroom and put on his pajamas, careful not to look at his flesh.

The soft parts would go first. The ones without bones. But which ones? His earlobes? The tip of his nose? His lips? Or...

He believed he could put her off for another night. But two nights in a row? She would be suspicious.

Still, he couldn't risk betraying himself in a fit of passion. That would be too sudden. He wanted the moment to be right. He wanted to break the news gently.

He rolled antiperspirant under his arms. Hairs came loose and clung to the deodorant ball. He splashed cologne on his neck. He was afraid to comb his hair.

"Randall?"

She was under the covers.

"Coming, dear," he answered.

He turned out the lights, not looking at the bed. He still had the gloves on. Silly boy.

"Silly boy," she said, feeling the gloves on her shoulders as he hugged her.

She was wearing lingerie, silk lace and frills. He rubbed the fabric against his cheek, lightly, so that his skin wouldn't slough. He missed having a sense of touch.

"Playing games tonight?" she whispered, a giggle in her nose.

"Not tonight, dear, I've..."

You've what?, he thought. Got a headache? Used that last night. Suffering the heartbreak of psoriasis? This morning's excuse.

"Honey?" she said, her voice husky with desire and disappointment.

"Tomorrow night, I promise," he said, in his most gentlemanly tone. It was the voice he used doing Laurence Olivier doing Hamlet.

He brushed his parched lips carefully against Demora's cheek. He nudged his nose against her ear. He tried to give her butterfly kisses, but his eyelids were too stiff.

Randall lay back on the pillows and pretended to sleep. He hoped she wouldn't put her head on his chest and notice the lack of a heartbeat. But soon she was snoring lightly, managing to turn even that into a song. His eyes remained open the entire night.

His blood had settled overnight as he lay in unsleep. The liver mortis mottled his skin. Getting out of bed was a chore. He just wanted to rest, rest, in peace.

But Demora needed him. This was no time to be selfish.

He dared not take the bus to work. He was drawing too many flies. His hands were too slow to brush them away. So he walked to work, his feet like mud in his shoes.

He looked at the sky, wide and blue over the tops of the buildings. He had never before noticed the breadth and depth of reality. The gray-chested pigeons hopping on the ledges, barren flagpoles erect in the air, awnings drooping like damp parachutes, shrubs rising from concrete boxes with cigarette butts for mulch. So much detail, every bit of mica in the sidewalk glistening in the sun, every flake of drab paint on the windowsills curling, all glass standing clear and thick and brittle and bold.

And the people, fat men with umbrellas, stalactite ladies with faux pearls, boys with big shoes, weasel women and pony girls. So many people, flush with health, cheeks blushed with blood, all hearts racing, pounding, pouring, pumping life. So alive. Such a treasure it was to breathe. The living knew not their wealth.

Randall pulled his derby lower over his face. He'd had to lighten the skin under his eyes with makeup. He had a kit at home. He'd done his own makeup for years, painting himself a hundred times to become someone else. He never thought he'd have to recreate his own face.

He entered the theater, his coat collar high around his ears even though the mercury was in the eighties. He had doused his clothes with a half-bottle of aftershave, but he didn't want to chance any personal encounters.

He waved at the stage director and went into his office. He took off his coat and sat in the chair. He tugged at the fingertip of his glove and heard a wet tearing sound. Probably the fingermeat was separating at his wedding band. He left the glove alone.

He stank. He knew that. Demora had not said a word. She would never criticize.

Randall sat. After a long eternity of hours that were all the same, the clock on the wall moved around. Time to go home, to Demora. He tried to rise.

He couldn't move. Rigor mortis had finally set in.

He had been wondering how long he could continue, how long he could pretend, how long he could fool himself and his Makers. Too many decades of smoking and lack of exercise.

Last Monday. Oh, what pain in his chest, a swollen river of fire, a smothering silence, a great white pillow of pressure on his head. That final sensation had been rich, screaming with the juice of nerves, as raw as birth and as bittersweet as the last day of autumn.

He winced at the memory. He had felt something lifting from his body, a powder, a fairy-dust, a star whisper. And he had resisted the pull.

Because of her.

And because of her, he could not sit locked in his chair, his muscles frozen around his skeleton, his face a tense mask, his eyes dry and bulging. He would not be found like this.

He summoned his willpower. He strained against invisible bonds. Finally, his jaw yanked downward.

He flexed his fingers, hearing his knuckles crack. He stood, his bones snapping like old sticks. He walked, his legs a daisy chain of calcite.

On the way home, he avoided looking into human eyes. He no longer envied their moistness. He no longer ached for tears. He had lost the desire to breathe, to live, to be normal. Living was just a state of mind.

Demora looked affectionately at him as she set the table. She tilted her head.

"Are you gaining weight, sweetheart?" she asked.

"No, dear."

He wasn't gaining. He was bloating.

Randall wore his hat while eating dinner. He wondered what was happening to the food now that his organs no longer digested. His gloves were stained with the cherry jubilee. Demora's lips were red, probably his as well.

He felt an urge to kiss her.

"Tonight, my love?" she said, looking deeply into his eyes.

"Yes," he answered. He lifted a toast in her direction. The Bourdeaux pooled in his dead stomach.

Did she suspect? He was pallid. He stank of loam and rancid meat. His skin was gelatin. His cheeks sagged from his skull. Flies orbited his head.

But he didn't think she minded. She loved him as he was, however he was. He saw it in her eyes.

Those fools had it wrong. All the great tragedies were based on a lie. Romeo and Juliet, hah.

Anybody could die for love. That was easy. The true test was living for love, afterwards.

Later, in bed, under sheets and midnight's rainbow, as candles flickered.

"I love you," Demora whispered.

"I love you, " Randall said, and he had never meant it so completely.

"Forever and for true?"

"Forever and a day."

He kissed her.

His mouth found new vigor.

His eyes moistened, as if brimming for weeping.

He felt stirrings below his belly.

His tongue writhed and squirmed in passion.

No, not his tongue.

Maggots.

Demora returned his kiss. Their limbs entwined, their flesh joined in a squishy, beautiful swapping of the juices of love. They drove their bodies toward satisfaction, but for Randall, the only fulfillment was in pleasing his wife.

By the time Randall had pulled away, bits of him were clinging to Demora. She endured without complaint. He hugged her into sleep. He stared unblinking at the ceiling, listening to the slow tick of the bedside clock and the gases expelling from his body. In the still air of dark night, the whole world was a coffin. Randall wondered if being dead would always be so endlessly, endlessly boring.

Finally, the sun reddened the window. Another day of being dead. Randall went to the bathroom and studied himself in the mirror. His eyes writhed with larvae. The softer meat of his face, the area around his eyes and lips, was dark as coal. The rest was shaded green, faintly moldy and mossy, down to his chest. He dared not look lower.

He turned on the shower, and the steam curled around him as he stepped under the nozzle. He welcomed the cleansing. The forceful jets of water dented his mottled skin, but he felt nothing. The flies spun in confused circles, their host lost in the scent of soap.

Bits of skin and flesh rained from his body. He stared between his rotted feet at the pieces of himself collecting in the drain. He spun the spigots until the water stopped. More of him fell away as he toweled himself dry.

"Honey?" Demora knocked on the bathroom door.

"I'm almost done." His voice was muffled by the insects that had spawned in his mouth.

"Coffee and toast, or would you rather have hot cereal?"

Randall couldn't face stuffing more tasteless food into his body. All he wanted was to pull his own eyelids down, to sleep, sleep. But Demora. She needed. He couldn't leave her all alone. He'd promised love eternal.

"I'm not hungry," he said, trying his best to sound cheerful. After all, they had made love last night. He ought to be in a good mood.

"Are you sure, dear?"

"Yes, I'm sure."

He reached for his bathrobe as her footsteps faded down the hall. He wrapped the terry cloth around him. Once the soft fabric would have comforted him. Now, it only reminded him of all he couldn't feel. He decided he would call in sick to work that day.

He went down the stairs, his feet slogging damply on the oak treads. The gloves, the makeup, the illusions were all useless now. The flesh under his jowls drooped in surrender to gravity and swung from side to side as he walked to the dinette. Demora whistled in the kitchen, an adagio operetta, her music accompanied by the percussion of cooking utensils. Randall slumped into a chair, beyond hope. If only he could die, finally and for real.

He straightened as Demora entered the room. Death wishes were selfish. He had made a promise. No force, from Beyond or otherwise, would make him yield before his duty was met.

Demora sat at the table across from him. Steam curled from her cup of coffee, a spirit of heat.

"We have to talk," she said, leaning forward. Her eyes narrowed and her lips tightened, the look she got when she was serious about something. He looked out the window at the green living world.

"It's a beautiful day," he said, "and I have a beautiful wife."

She almost smiled. "That's sweet, but you're changing the subject."

"What subject?" A piece of his lip plopped onto the table. A maggot writhed in the black meat.

"You're keeping something from me."

"Me?" He tried to open his eyes in feigned innocence, but he had no eyelids.

"We've always been honest with each other..."

"Of course, dear."

"...and I can tell when something's bothering you."

"Nothing's bothering me." Newly-born flies spilled from his mouth along with his words. The flies' wings were shiny in the morning light.

"Don't lie to me, honey."

Yes, lying was futile. She could always read him like a book.

"I can tell you're unhappy," she continued. He raised his hand to protest. The white bones of his fingers showed through in places.

"And nothing would pain me more than for you to be unhappy," Demora said. Those lips, those kind, serious eyes. He was never more sure of anything than he was of her undying love.

"Is it selfish of me?" he asked. "To refuse to let go?"

"No, I'm the selfish one. I'm holding you here when your heart is leading you in another direction."

"For better or worse. That was my vow to you."

"Till death do us part. That was also your vow."

Her eyes welled with tears. So he had hurt her, despite all his effort and will, despite his defiance of nature. He couldn't bear to hurt her.

She nodded at him. He understood. She was releasing him, granting him permission to die for her. He had been wrong. The supreme sacrifice was hers, not his.

"I'm so very tired," he whispered.

She reached across the table, gripping his decaying hands in hers. His wedding ring clacked against bone.

"I love you," he said, feeling his soul lifting and leaking away, wafting from his putrid corpse to mingle with the sky.

"I know," she answered, her voice breaking. "Forever and a day."

Even the day after forever had to end. His heart was light, buoyant with relief and freed now from the cages of the flesh. His last sensation was of Demora's hands squeezing good-bye, urging him onward, giving her blessing to his departure. He had fulfilled his vows, and all that remained was to find peace.

And wait for Demora.

After Words

This is the fun part for the author, but can be dreadfully tedious for some readers. So I will certainly forgive you if you close the book now, content that I have adequately rewarded you for your investment of time, money, and spiritual trust. If I haven't contented you yet, then I doubt these after words will finish the job, but perhaps the "story behind the story" can prove a nourishing dessert to what I hope was an engaging feast.

Here's how these stories happened:

"Haunted"

I wrote this story in the summer of 1998. As usual, I wasn't sure exactly what I was trying to say. It started with the idea of "What if ghosts are themselves haunted?"

The story appeared in the *More Monsters From Memphis* anthology, and was later reprinted in the e-zine *Electric Wine*. It's been called everything from a time travel story to what one newspaper critic called "a story so profound in its sense of doom and loss that the reader's own life is elevated in comparison." It placed as First Runner-Up for the 1998 Darrell Award and received an Honorable Mention in *Year's Best Fantasy & Horror*.

"The Vampire Shortstop"

There are moments in this life when everything falls into place, when you go beyond your abilities, when good ideas teleport themselves into your brain without your knowledge. So it was with this story. I awoke one morning with the words "vampire shortstop" in my head. It was probably one of those puns that the sleepy subconscious likes to make, the play on "vampire" and "umpire."

I went straight to my keyboard and wrote this story practically at one sitting. The whole time, my fingers were racing over the keys, and I kept telling myself, "Don't interfere, don't pay attention, don't get in the way of this gift from wherever, don't dare inflict any writerisms on this thing." I was on automatic pilot, what I call "ghost-writing," when the story is doing a fine job of telling itself with no help from me.

The story won the 1998 L. Ron Hubbard Gold Award and was published in the *Writers of the Future Volume XV*. It was reprinted in the anthology *Baseball Fantastic*, edited by W.P. Kinsella. I coach Little League during those seasons when my schedule allows, and the coach in the story is about as close to autobiography as I've ever come.

"Skin"

This story was published in the Canadian anthology *Northern Horror* in 2000 despite a very American problem centered on health-care costs. "Skin" went though several drafts as I tried to develop the protagonist's character, to impart a reason for why this bad thing was happening to this particular person. Why should we care whether this greedy, petty miser gets haunted by a skin donor?

Revenge stories are usually tiresome and trite, but I hope this story goes beyond that, to make you wonder what happens to a person's soul when the various parts are parceled off. I'm signed up as an organ donor myself, but if you somehow end up with a piece of me, I promise not to come back to retrieve my organs.

"Dead Air"

This was a mystery story I wrote while attending Appalachian State University in 1996. I was working at the college radio station at the time, and it's sometimes convenient to "write what you know." It's a fairly straight-forward story, but I like the main character. Maybe there's a little lesson about the media promoting violence in there, but it's wholly unintentional, this is a work of fiction, actual mileage may vary, etc. It originally appeared in *Blue Murder Magazine* #3 in 1997.

"In The Heart Of November"

I wrote this for a young adult anthology published by Tundra Books in Canada. Thanks go to Edo van Belkom for editing assistance on this one. The difference between writing for a younger audience and writing for adults is that, to those not yet jaded by the years, the emotional stakes are so much higher. Love and death are always ripe territory for literary exploration.

"The Three-Dollar Corpse"

This story marked a couple of milestones for me. It was the first time a story of mine sold on its first trip through the postage, and it also made liberal use of the fruits of research. I read several personal accounts by Civil War soldiers who had been imprisoned at the infamous Andersonville camp in Georgia. Those details were so rich, so hauntingly resonant, that they brought this story to life for me.

The title comes from the practice of prisoners selling the right to carry bodies out for burial, because getting outside the gates allowed one to trade or buy enough goods to survive until the next day's funeral procession. Fiction can never match the true horrors that exist in this world. "The Three-Dollar Corpse" made its first appearance in the anthology *Dead Promises* in 1999.

"Thirst"

"Thirst" is a change of pace from many of the other stories. The fantasy is of a lighter quality, and again explores the turmoils and joys of childhood. The "style" is an unabashed imitation of Ray Bradbury, but, of course, falls far short of that man's literary magic. My penalty for trying to foster a "style"? I must write ten thousand times, "I shall not extend metaphors as if they were my precious writerly arms."

This story was first published in German, at a website called *Storisende* and later in the anthology *Die Drachen Von Morgan.*

"Do You Know Me Yet?"

I got the idea for this story after meeting British horror writer Ramsey Campbell at a writer's convention. I'd just read his story called "Next Time You'll Know Me," in which a character stalks writers who he thinks are stealing his ideas. I thought it would be amusing if someone accused Mr. Campbell of stealing the idea for *that* story.

The story also pokes a little fun at the horror genre and some of its biggest writers. Strangely, the anthology containing this story (*The Asylum: The Psycho Ward*, 1999) came out scant days after Stephen King was seriously injured after being struck by a van. I felt a little bad at the time, but I trust Mr. King is secure enough to laugh at such minor gnat-bites as mine. If not, he's welcome to stalk me in order to get his revenge. Or he can send George Stark after me.

"Homecoming"

I don't know how many different versions of this story I've written. It began in a college writing class, and was almost universally panned by my fellow students. I knew something was in there, though, something that kept calling me back, something that wanted to be brought to life and then buried with honor. I finally realized that this was Charlie's story, not mine, so I let him have it.

"Homecoming" was originally published in 1998 by *Maelstrom*, a small-press magazine based in North Carolina. After the story was published, I found a different, longer version that I'd completely forgotten about. Good. I don't see how that excess verbiage could have added anything. And Charlie is a man of few words, anyway.

"Kill Your Darlings"

At long last, a rather happy ending. The title is from something William Faulkner supposedly said, though I've heard it attributed to one or two other "great writers." The idea is that a writer must cut out every precious little phrase, no matter how elegant and beautiful, if that phrase does not advance the story.

Okay, okay, another story with a writer as protagonist. You're only supposed to get one your entire career, and I've included two in this book. So shoot me.

Uh, on second thought...

First published in *Blue Murder Magazine* #5 in 1997. It's actually one of the first stories I wrote after beginning my "serious" career as a writer, meaning that I became determined to write daily, or at least feel guilty if I didn't.

"Metabolism"

This is the first story I ever sold. It was a finalist in the Writers of the Future contest, and editor Dave Wolverton called me one January evening to say he wanted to publish the story in the anthology *Writers of the Future Volume XIV*, along with the contest prize-winners.

After I hung up, I went upstairs to the room where I was doing my writing at the time. I took down all of the rejection slips I had faithfully pinned to my bulletin board. I counted them. One-hundred-and-five. I sat down, held that awesomely humiliating stack, and thought about the thousand hours I had spent in that room in the past year, straining over the keyboard, my gut clenched in conflict, my eyes dry from strain, my brain long since numbed to rejection. I asked myself, "Was it worth it?"

Oh yes. Most certainly yes.

"The Boy Who Saw Fire"

"The Boy Who Saw Fire" is more of a descriptive set piece than a traditional story. I wrote this in 1997, and sent it off to The Leading Edge, a fiction digest published by students at Brigham Young University. I forgot about it until I received a letter over a year later saying they wanted to publish it. The story came out in #36, September 1998.

"The Boy Who Saw Fire" is based on the same mythical world as "Thirst." Maybe I'll go back someday and check in on Billy when we both get a little older.

"Constitution"

This story, I hope, sums up the theme I tried to establish with this collection. I wanted to have a unified flavor to the book, so I purposely omitted my science fiction and some of my more edgy dark fantasy. This story first appeared in *Carpe Noctem* in 1999. *Carpe Noctem* bills itself as a "death-positive" magazine.

Death positive. That's interesting, and oddly optimistic. There's so much negativity in the world, so many artfully-posing gloomies who herald a coming doomsday. Well, we know we're going to die. So what? To me, courage is not found in celebrating a black void. Courage is in continuing to love, to build, to believe in spite of it.

All religious tenets respectfully aside, I truly believe that love is stronger than time, death, decay, fear, or words. Love is the single greatest gift, the most cosmic power, the thing most worthy of sacrifice in this world. Love is life, and cannot be destroyed. So why shouldn't love defeat the emptiness and bleakness of the grave?

Hope should never surrender, and love should never rest in peace.

Thank you for the flowers you have brought me, the flowers of your trust and dreams and faith, plucked from the garden of your soul. Thank you for sharing the colors of your heart. Thank you for breathing with me.